THE CANARY
AND OTHER TALES OF MARTIAL LAW

THE CANARY
AND OTHER TALES OF MARTIAL LAW

MAREK NOWAKOWSKI

Translated by Krystyna Bronkowska

With a preface by Leszek Kolakowski

The Dial Press
DOUBLEDAY AND COMPANY, INC.
GARDEN CITY, NEW YORK
1984

Published by The Dial Press

First published in Polish as *Raport o stanie wojennym*
by Institut Litteraire, Paris 1982 and 1983

First published in the English language
by Harvill Press, 1983
© Institut Litteraire Paris & Marek Nowakowski,
1982 and 1983
Translation © Harvill Press, 1983

Library of Congress Cataloging in Publication Data

Nowakowski, Marek.
The canary and other tales of martial law.

"First published in Polish as Raport o stanie wojennym
by Institut Litteraire, Paris 1982 and 1983."—p. iv.
1. Poland—History—1980– —Fiction.   I. Title.
PG7173.0'83R3613   1984   891.8'537   83-45562
ISBN 0-385-27988-4

Contents

————————— * —————————

Preface

-----*-----

This is not strictly speaking a collection of short stories. They are rather snapshots taken in haste a few weeks after the so-called martial law, or rather lawlessness, had been declared in Poland on 13 December 1981. As in all his books, Nowakowski stays as close as possible to rough everyday experience without diluting it by psychological explanations or imposing on it his own abstract judgements. If people argue against each other on political or philosophical issues, their discussions remain on the level which directly touches the most elementary aspects of their lives and is expressed in that inimitable urban slang that so strangely mixes cynicism with despair, contempt for principles with belief in principles. Nowakowski's characters often come from the so-called 'social margin', but in a communist country this particular category has lost any distinctive meaning, as everybody in one sense or another belongs to the 'social margin' and all genuine human bonds are built outside, and more often than not against, the official structure of the society.

The gap between real society and the imaginary country depicted in the official jargon of communism has never been so grotesquely wide in the history of Poland. The sixteen-month-long period of Solidarity was a great effort to give the real country a kind of visible and institutional existence, thereby limiting the omnipotence of the police state. The aim of the Soviet-sponsored coup which imposed on Poland a military dictatorship was to destroy the

7

spontaneously emerging movement of workers, intellectuals, and peasants and to restore the unlimited and uncontrolled power of the communist bureaucracy. The coup, officially called 'the state of war', was quite successful in technical terms and proved an abysmal failure in any other sense. The Communist Party has remained in its old state of rigor mortis, the economic catastrophe has not been reversed, and the conspiratorial Solidarity has not been crushed despite countless trials, repression, beatings, and even murders: the mass of hatred is growing to an unprecedented degree.

Though they might seem to be selected at random, the pictures collected in Nowakowski's ugly album together make a very convincing panorama of the first weeks of the 'war' declared on Poland by a clique of generals. Conspirators and stool-pigeons, cowards and fighters, deep in despair and deep in hope, police thugs and reluctant soldiers – they do not seem to have much in common except that all of them, both the rapists and the raped, know exactly what is at stake and what the 'war' is for: what matters is not communism or socialism, not an idea, not a social order, and not economic problems, but a mortal fear of the privileged clique which suddenly realized that the power they were given by a foreign empire might not last forever.

DR LESZEK KOLAKOWSKI
All Souls College, Oxford
June 1983

8

The State of War [1]

——————————*——————————

Darkness had fallen. The cold was intense. The suburb had emptied earlier than usual. The only sound was a metallic clanking from the black fortress-like mass of the steelworks. Tanks and transporters were moving up to the barricaded gates. The army was about to surround the plant. A column of infantry marched behind the tanks. Glints of cold steel as their bayonets caught the sparse lamplight. Concrete blocks barred the road. Two soldiers in caps with earflaps stood guard. They stamped their feet and clapped their hands. Their Kalashnikovs were slung across their chests. Coke glowed in a brazier on the other side of the barrier. A third sentry was warming himself by it. He stirred the red embers with a rod.

Long icicles hung from the house roofs. As sharp as daggers. The sentry stood clear of the factory wall with its dangerous bristling fringe. And the rare passers-by carefully kept their distance. The soldier's eyes followed each one, watchfully, his hands abandoning the warmth to rest on the Kalashnikov. People hurried across the road, staring straight ahead. The windows of tenements were dark, looked lifeless. It was the third day of the war. Nearly curfew time.

A taxi came out of a side road. Approached the barrier. Stopped at the concrete blocks. The soldiers closed in, machine guns at the ready. A document check. They

[1] The Polish term for martial law means literally 'state of war', and is often shortened to 'the war'.

9

opened the boot and rummaged in it. The taxi turned around and went back.

The silence was now complete. The armoured vehicles had stopped their clanking.

For quite a time no-one came into view. When the clatter of footsteps came it sounded unduly loud. Someone was shuffling along slowly and heavily. An ungainly hunchback figure loomed dimly in the gateway, hobbled towards the brazier. An old woman with a sack over her shoulder. The young soldier gave her a careful look. She dropped her burden on the ground. Her face was thin, lined, hollow. Grey strands of hair fell from under her headscarf. Her hands stretched over the fire.

'You must be cold, soldier?' She crouched over the brazier, eyes half closed.

A siren sounded from the steelworks. Tore up the frozen silence. The sentries in the roadway moved uneasily. The young soldier looked up. The old woman didn't stir. She seemed more dead than alive. But the hands were still held over the fire. The fingers, misshapen with arthritis, trembled unceasingly. The young soldier stirred impatiently. The old hag was a nuisance. He cleared his throat, looked pointedly at his watch. The old woman's head moved grudgingly upward.

'The pity of it. I'm sorry for everybody. You as well, soldier.' The voice sounded thin, used up. The eyes fixed on his might have belonged to his mother. But they were also the piercing eyes of a hawk.

'Look, soldier! Blood on the snow.'

The young soldier was taken aback. Looked on the ground around. The snow shone, white, untouched, immaculate. He shuddered. The cold was getting worse. But the old woman's words were icier still. And she stared at him so fixedly.

'Come off it, grannie!' he said at last, his hands automatically moving to the Kalashnikov slung across his chest. He had a round peasant face. He looked down again and furrowed the snow with the toe of his boot.

The old woman lifted up her beggar's sack. Shuffled off. Vanished into the dark. For a while he could still hear the snow crunching under her feet.

'Who goes there?' called one of the soldiers on guard outside the works.

'Some daft old woman,' the young soldier called back. After a pause. He squatted by the fire again and the coke crackled. Fire, smoke . . .

1 January 1982

The Night Patrol

———————————— * ————————————

They were taking a risk, starting to queue at a quarter to six. There had been an alert from the butcher's: they were supposed to be bringing beef, pork, and giblets. A big delivery, rumour had it. It worked like a magnet: before the end of curfew, the queue was quite long. Mostly old women and pensioners. If there was trouble, no-one would touch the old people. Or so they hoped. Some younger men booked places in the queue but hid in a nearby gateway for the time being. They chain-smoked, on the lookout all the time. Not that you could see much in the half light. Most streetlamps had been turned off to save electricity and a thick fog had come down. It was cold. The fog promised another snow-fall. The old people in the queue waited, calm and unafraid.

'They can't touch me,' gasped one old man with a wheezing cough. He started pulling out papers to show that he had fought at Lenino, had been decorated twice, and was a member of the Ex-Combatants' Association.

Just as he stopped boasting, the measured tramp of boots on crackling snow was heard. They were coming from the square by the Palace of Weddings. A few of the nimbler old people ran to join the younger set in the gateway. The rest stayed put. The night patrol approached the queue. Four of them. Three with rifles and one in front with a revolver in an open holster. Their torches lit up the queue squatting against the wall. The patrol stopped.

'What's all this about?' said the one in front. No answer.

He glanced at his watch. 'Another thirty-five minutes to go.'

'Please let us off, captain,' an old woman's voice whined. The officer in charge waited fully a minute.

'We shall take the names of all those in breach of regulations,' he said at last, 'and send them before a tribunal.' His torch shed bright light on face after face in the queue. The dazzled eyes blinked. His gloves now off, the officer drew out a notebook.

'We'll start at the head of the queue. Those in front were the first to contravene the regulations.'

'Please let us off, captain,' screeched the same female voice.

The officer ignored her. He started hauling people out of the queue one by one. Each was taken aside and briefly detained. They were then allowed to return to their places in the queue. Most kept silent, but one of those who had been processed managed to breathe out:

'He'll take two hundred.'

Those further down the queue now knew what was expected and had the necessary notes ready.

He got through the lot in a matter of minutes. He never even looked in the gateway where the young were hiding. Finally, the notebook went back into its case. He fastened the straps carefully, and was ready to move on. His men were finishing their cigarettes.

'What about the next patrol?' the ex-combatant plucked up his courage to ask. 'Won't they expect to collect?'

'What did you say?' the officer asked, looking surprised, and signalled to his men.

They marched away.

The queue was still there, the same length as before. Comment on the event was meagre and subdued. Some thought it was the militia. Others thought the army. Opinion was divided. The darkness had thinned. Ten minutes to go till the end of curfew. Snow started falling, fine but fast.

The Taxi Driver's Story

—————————— * ——————————

The best thing for a frozen lock is brake fluid. Pour a few drops in, and turn the key. Or warm it up. This morning I had to go through this lock routine again. But the engine started straightaway and the day wasn't too bad. There aren't many taxis about, you see. Petrol for us private cabbies is scarce but I bought some on the side from the army. They camp in the wood just behind us to keep an eye on the factory. A whole column of transporters. Hungry and cold they are. Some soldiers got into the confectioner's on our estate and finished off all the cakes. In no time at all. Passengers don't talk much nowadays. People are afraid of one another. The snitches are bound to come out on top again. Nosing about, winning prizes for vigilance. I gave a ride to one myself. Fur hat, beefy red face, Mongol-looking. I watched him in the mirror. The twister was there to check up on me.

'Well, we'll have peace and order at last.'

'I beg your pardon?'

'Oh, so you don't agree with me?'

'Beg pardon,' I repeated, 'I'm hard of hearing. Eardrums gone.'

He made a face and looked me up and down. End of conversation. I got rid of him on Pulawska Street in the square near the police reservation. Hurrying to work, probably. There's one checkpoint after another round there. All cars are stopped, everybody is checked. HQ, military government.

14

Fares come in all shapes. Some still talk:
'Did you know the militia had a special ration for Christmas? They've lifted all the carp from the palace lake. About half a ton, they say. The best carp, royal fish.' I must have looked surprised. 'Well, what do you expect?' he went on. 'They've worked hard enough, haven't they, those lads?'

This one wasn't trying it on. I could tell. He was one of us. Had a drawn-out, hacking cough. Too much vodka.

'They'll kill the swans off next.' He broke a fag in two and put one half in a glass holder. Smokers have it rough. The ration doesn't go anywhere.

Some still talk just as they did before. Their mouths haven't gummed up yet. Most don't. In no mood for it. They keep their heads down. When our eyes meet in the mirror, they look away. They all have their troubles and vexations. Friends, family arrested, interned. Take this old couple. She talked all the time, about her internment. The camp, the wire, roll calls, cells. The old man did his best with her.

'Quiet now, quiet dear . . .' He stroked her hand again and again. To me he said that her nerves had given up. They were on their way to the loony bin. This war takes people different ways. An old person like that remembers the other war, the Occupation, the executions, the round-ups. It had all bounced back at her. Nothing surprising in that. I've had fares wearing black crepe bands on their sleeves, in mourning because of the state of war. The young come through best. One bloke, in an American combat jacket, asked me at the end of the ride:

'Do you know this one? CROW may try but Eagle flies high.'[1] And he burst out laughing.

Just as well the young hold on. There's some hope that way, a future of sorts. But you can't get the black thoughts

[1] WRONA, the acronym for the ruling Council of Military Salvation, the Junta, is also Polish for crow. The white eagle is, of course, the Polish national symbol.

out of your head. You try to shake them off, but they stick like burrs to a dog's tail. The cold is cruel. The old are going under, a lot of funerals about. With telephones cut off, you never get an ambulance in time. Streets full of tanks, police vans, all sorts of army vehicles. Gangs of militia, swarming, nosing. Enough to choke you. Mustn't let it get you down. Easier said than done, though.

They stopped my taxi five times today. First the licence, then the meter. They searched the car. The last check really upset me. On my way home, hoping for a fare going my way.

'Stop!'

Soldiers in quilted jackets, caps with earflaps, Kalashnikovs at the ready, frozen, stamping their feet. Gumboots in this weather!

'Documents!' Their fingers were so stiff that they couldn't turn the pages.

'Cold, those boots,' I said.

'They have linings. But they are cold all the same,' said the soldier.

'The militia', I observed, 'have decent felt boots.'

He said nothing.

The corporal on the other side poked his head in.

'Open the passenger door!'

I did. He rummaged under the seat. What did he expect, I ask you? A bomb? A load of gelignite? He didn't find it. I started the engine.

'Hold on a minute. Let's have a look underneath.' He knelt down, and stuck his head under the cab. A lump of frozen snow got him under the collar. His cap fell off. When he got up, his face was all mucky with oil. I could hardly keep a straight face.

'Now the boot,' barked my corporal.

I pressed the button. He saw the spare wheel and the tools. Nothing else. Come on, you bloodhound you! A bit of work will do you good in this cold. As he slammed the boot, it sprang open. He did it again. It opened again . . . You have to know my boot. There's a knack to it. He kept banging the lid and every time it bounced back again. The corporal was puffing and panting. Down, up, down, up, bang, bang, bang.

I lit a fag.

'Hold on. You're wrecking the lid, citizen corporal.'

He gave me a look but not a word.

I leant on the steering wheel and watched calmly. I switched the radio on. Sweet music filled the air.

Keen as he was, he had to give up in the end. Asked me to help.

'Here's how you do it. But did you have to go on like that, mate?'

He exploded.

'Damn it, d'you think this is all my idea?'

There's hope for that bloke yet.

The Secret Face

———————✳———————

The new boss (called himself the administrator) arrived and declared our union suspended. A small man, watery eyes and a voice to match. From you-know-which department. Smoked Carmen. Crept around with our manager telling him what was to be sealed off and what could go on working. The canteen and the pay office were OK. They could dispense grants and allowances already passed, and also thin broth and Ukrainian dumplings. Ukrainian dumplings are what we've usually had lately. The doctor could go on seeing patients in his room. Some of the women cried a bit. Especially those who've been in the office for a long time. One of the old ladies got so upset that she had to take a heart pill.

We'd never had our union suspended before. Not since 1945, anyway. The older women must have felt this was the end. The administrator went from room to room, with the women trailing behind him like wet hens. Stopped every time he stopped. Their eyes blankly followed his every move. Couldn't believe what they saw, I suppose. Yet you only had to take a look through the window. There was a tank at the church door. A sight not seen since the war. Its gun was pointing at the castle clock. On the opposite corner there was an army checkpoint. Soldiers, guns at the ready, busy stopping cars.

'I must say,' said Felek, our driver, '– I must say they know their job, the army! Here, there, and everywhere!'

No-one knew what he meant by it. Felek is a bit daft.

18

Just back from his army service. Still in his camouflage jacket.

'Now then, the minutes. Where are they kept?' asked the administrator.

The manager thought deeply. The women kept mum. So did we all. Our little game didn't work. Citizen Piotrowska – or Lula, as she likes to be called. 'Call me Lula,' she would simper, and smack a wet kiss on your face. She'd been in the office less than a year but she was Lula to everyone – Citizen Piotrowska took over.

'There!' Pointing to a small cabinet. Under the picture of our first president.

'Yes, I see,' mumbled the administrator. And asked for the key. The manager searched his pockets. He couldn't find it. Nobody could. But Lula knew where the keys were. She took herself off to the manager's office with the administrator for a private talk. The manager had just time to breathe:

'The Solidarity papers, get them away.'

Bozenka, our Solidarity delegate, pushed it all into a wastepaper bin – and ran! Our cloakroom attendant, a smart old girl, had hiding places of her own. 'They can go on looking for weeks,' she said. So the papers were safe, at least. A minute or two later Lula and the administrator emerged from the office. You could see there was already something between them. A bond of mutual confidence. They exchanged discreet whispers, Lula nodding eager assent. Openly flirting with him. Leading him on. She got herself a job. Cataloguing the union records. She ordered Bozenka to type the thing: 'I'll dictate it to you.'

She looked daggers at us all. There was such defiance in her eyes, such arrogance. This wasn't the Lula we knew. The mask was off. Even our manager snorted in disgust. We knew for a fact there used to be something between him and Piotrowska. The messenger had walked in on them once and had to back out double quick. They were up against the desk. All over each other. 'There was the manager, handling her big tits,' he told us with a snigger. 'They'll be getting down to it on the office carpet any minute.'

He was good with his gestures, too.

But the manager was really pissed off now. With a bit of luck, Lula would be in business with the administrator any second now. The manager could probably picture it: the carpet by his desk, and those two alone there . . .

While we were mulling over Lula's metamorphosis, our book-keeper suddenly spoke up. He's reached retirement age, so he doesn't give a shit. They can't touch him. He's a big tall fellow, ex-cavalryman. He stood up stiff as a ramrod and addressed Lula in his boozy baritone:

'I see, citizen, that you now have a position of trust here . . .'

Piotrowska stuck her chest out even further. She's a buxom piece. Breasts like pumpkins. Quite mouthwatering, really.

'What's that to you? Don't you like it?'

The book-keeper went on, 'That's neither here nor there. Only . . . my dear Lula, haven't you shown your hand too early? Are you sure of the odds?'

He left it at that, and turned to the window, to contemplate the military scene outside the church.

He had upset her all right. Would you believe it: she stood stock-still with her mouth wide open, and nothing came out. Some confused activity was going on inside her head.

The clanking and whirring of tanks could be heard from the street. The book-keeper had had his fill. He turned round again. Gave us all a look. Kindly, but detached.

'More of you will show their true faces in due course,' the old bastard drawled.

We couldn't help eyeing one another. The poisoned seed had been sown.

Our manager gave the administrator a jerky bow and left the room.

The Canary

———————————*———————————

Kubus was very old.

'We're in the same way, Kubus and I,' grandma would say. She treated the canary as a partner with equal rights.

She always knew whether he was in a good humour or not. She could tell from the look in his eyes. She did all she could to please him. It was to him that she addressed her long monologues, with their unexpected punch lines. The way his beak moved, the way his filmy eyes opened and shut, conveyed to her his approval or dissent.

'You're right, Kubus, of course,' she would say, 'but what else could I do?'

Her stories were concerned, more often than not, with the remote past. They went back to her youth, her school-days in St Petersburg, her adventures during the First World War and the Russian Revolution.

Listening to the canary's morning song was grandma's greatest pleasure. He would hop to the top of the cage and strike up there. Grandma sat facing him, and listened with religious concentration. If someone suddenly came into the room, grandma's finger went to her lips, commanding silence. In her mind, Kubus was an outstanding performer, a Caruso among canaries. The purity of his voice, his high register, and the richness of his tunes were often the subject of our telephone conversations.

No wonder grandma got upset when, one morning, he failed to perform. Difficult at the best of times, Kubus now just ruffled his feathers and pecked fiercely at the finger grandma proffered.

'There, there, Kubus,' said grandma, trying to soothe him. She hoped against hope that his silence might be only a passing whim. But next morning there was still no sound. Kubus had ceased to sing.

'It's like a house in mourning,' announced grandma on the telephone, and those words described exactly the state she was in. She never took her eyes off the canary, who dozed with his head tucked under his wing. She wondered anxiously whether he was ill, and we discussed arrangements for taking him to an animal clinic. The proclamation of martial law postponed all that.

We just forgot about it. We visited grandma occasionally to take her some vital provisions and to exchange anxious and chaotic thoughts on the sad events in our country. Grandma was even more put out than we were. For one thing, when the telephones were cut off, she lost her only contact with other people. Because of her rheumatism she hardly ever left the flat. She spent her days gazing in helpless reproach at two objects in her room: the silent telephone and the cage with its silent canary. All this, and of course her experiences in the past, made grandma pessimistic.

'The Soviet Union is like a snake,' she would pronounce, as if in a clairvoyant trance. 'It promises and promises and then it strikes and strangles you.'

We hadn't visited grandma for some days when they finally reconnected the telephones in our town. Grandma rang us first. The call was preceded by a monotonously repetitive taped announcement: 'This conversation is being monitored. This conversation is being monitored.' It put grandma off for a second or so, but she waited for the refrain to cease, got her connection, and shouted joyfully into the receiver.

'Would you believe it, the canary is singing again!'

There was a click on the line and a voice, live this time, addressed grandma sternly:

'No code, please, or we shall disconnect you at once.'

Grandma was most indignant.

'The man's off his head! I can't put it more plainly. The canary has started singing again.'

There was another click and she really was disconnected. She tried to dial again, jiggled the receiver in its cradle. Dead silence. Cut off from the world. Still, Kubus was singing. That meant a great deal. We took grandma along to the local council office. We had a letter from the Residents' Committee, to say that the canary really existed. We joined a long queue, and grandma stood patiently leaning on two sticks.

'I went all through the revolution in Russia,' she said, 'and then the Red Terror, but there was never anything like this . . .'

We tried to quieten her down. She was indignant.

'What do you mean, "Keep quiet"?'

We waited for it.

'"No code", indeed!' Grandma raised her voice. 'The man is off his head!'

People in the queue turned to look at us.

The Washing Machine
--------------------------------*--------------------------------

That's when it started. On that memorable Sunday, 13 December. My wife had an understanding with her. We'd been borrowing her washing machine for a long time. Of course, we have our names down for one of our own but it's a long wait. Thousands on the list. She got hers through the army. Her late husband was a regular soldier, a sergeant. Well, then, I knocked on her door to get the key to the wash-house. She kept the machine there. I knocked and knocked. The radio was blaring, full on. Somebody making a speech. We always have a lie-in on Sundays and don't listen to the news till midday.

She opened the door at last.

'Come in, neighbour. Come in.'

She's hospitable. I'll give her that.

That's when I learnt about this state of war. It was the general speaking. I must admit I was dumbstruck. And there she was, that woman, dancing round the room and repeating:

'The army has taken over! The army has taken over!' over and over again.

I forgot about the key.

'Coffee?' she asked.

I refused.

'Isn't his voice nice? So deep and so warm!'

I looked at her and couldn't believe my eyes.

The old hag had positively blossomed.

'My son should be back soon. We're off to the cemetery to see my husband's grave.'

25

She made a suitably sad widow's face. But she was not in mourning for long. She started humming a song in a tuneless, worn-out voice.

I felt my hackles rising. I left the flat as fast as I could. The officers' whore! There was no other name for her. Not, incidentally, of my invention.

I remember that husband of hers, the sergeant, very well. A quiet, self-contained man. But every now and then came a day of reckoning. He would get home drunk, spoiling for a fight. We live next door, so we heard every word. The sergeant chucked the furniture about and swore. It was on one of those occasions that I heard the vulgar term 'officers' whore'. That's what he called his lawful wedded wife. He also roughed her up at times, and for days afterwards she would have to wear dark glasses. He broke her nose once. He looked a quiet, polite sort of chap. DIY enthusiast, mended taps, electrical gadgets. Before they moved into our block they'd spent years in barracks and camps. They'd met in some such place – in the officers' mess. She never failed to stress that. Liked you to know that she'd had swarms of admirers around her. All officers, of course. So she treated her husband with some disdain. He was just an NCO. He, on the other hand, must have remembered her preference for the higher ranks. Till the day he died, a colossal row took place at least once a month. He died of a coronary. Gave up the ghost in the ambulance on the way to hospital.

Financially, she was OK. Had a widow's pension from the army and a son who took good care of her, I must admit. He managed to organize all sorts of extras for her: furniture straight from the factory, carpets. The son is also an army man. A captain. I can't say what branch he's in. They have their perks, the boys in power, even when they don't thieve. What was that to me? Nothing, of course. But the war has been going on a month now and the old hag has really gone off her rocker. Among other things, she is in love with the military man who reads the news on the television.

'So handsome! That sulky look! And his features, so regular!'

Enough to drive you crazy. I watch her crossing her legs covered with varicose veins, her hair crimped, cheap scent smelling to high heaven. She stares at the telly for hours. The screen is filled with the military nowadays. They orate, opine, discuss. She sits transfixed. And the general has everything, in her opinion: looks, mysterious charm, charisma. It's not only my wife and I: all the neighbours are fed up. Even the party members. But that's not all: she has taken to going for walks. There's an army post near the viaduct. The soldiers warm themselves by a coke fire. Soldiers and militia. She comes close. Tries to draw their attention. Giggles, grins. The soldiers are quite nice to her. They desperately need a bit of friendliness. Normally, a wall of silence cuts them off from the rest of us. It isn't really their fault. Duty is duty. She was chased away once – by the militia, not the soldiers. Not that she knows the difference. They told her quite roughly:

'Go home and be quick about it!'

She was most indignant but still walked away swinging whatever she had left to swing. And she was back the next morning! Brought them sweets and biscuits.

'Why don't you pop in for a cup of coffee?'

She has no shame. What can you do with a woman like that? Shave her head? She hasn't much hair left, a few reddish wisps, you can see her scalp. It's the nature of the beast.

But, things being as they are, I've told my wife categorically that we mustn't borrow the washer any more.

Enough is enough!

On the Bus

—————— ✳ ——————

Bus No. 122 was going down Belvederska Street. The passengers sat in silence. Of late, people tend to sit in silence on buses. None of the arguments, none of the jokes you used to get. The bus braked sharply at a crossing but even that failed to provoke a comment. A ribbon of army transporters and lorries unwound while the bus waited. Guns wobbled under tarpaulins. A Gazik brought up the rear. As soon as the convoy had passed, the bus moved forward cautiously over the icy asphalt. It passed the 'colony', a row of buildings of differing heights surrounded by a wall, housing Russian diplomats and advisers.

'Walled themselves in, the Russkis!' said a nondescript young man in a fur hat which had seen better days. 'Must be afraid of an attack.'

His voice was surprisingly loud and penetrating. He ended with a crazy sort of giggle.

A few passengers looked at the walled quarters. Nobody spoke.

'What was that you said?' Another voice, from the front of the bus. A fat squat man. Good fur hat, face shiny, clean shaven. He elbowed his way towards the young man, who was standing by the middle door.

The young man looked put out. He glanced instinctively at the door.

The driver was watching the incident in his mirror. Suddenly he jammed on his brakes, then accelerated just as abruptly. The standing passengers were precipitated to the front, taking the fat man in the fur hat with them. He resisted, but was swept along by an avalanche of bodies and pinned to the glass partition dividing the driver's cab from the passengers.

A momentary smile appeared on the driver's tired, unshaven face. It vanished at once. He drove on, concentrating on the icy surface.

The fat man in the fur hat struggled to get free but to no avail. He gripped the back of a seat with both hands and tried to push himself forward. Managed to move a bit but got stuck at a seat for the disabled. The cripple sitting there held his stiff leg fully extended across the aisle.

A request stop. The forward thrust of all those bodies immobilized the fat man in the fur hat. The driver pressed a button. The automatic doors opened with a hiss. The middle door first. The nondescript young man, who was standing right by the steps, jumped out nimbly.

The fat man in the fur hat laboriously fought his way towards the door at the front. He was at some disadvantage. A raging, red-faced bulldog. The driver watched him coolly, waited politely. The fat man made it in the end. Once outside he peered helplessly in every direction. The young man was nowhere to be seen. He took down the number of the departing bus.

2072 Days

————————————— * —————————————

Stubborn as a mule, he always was.

'You won't make it, you and your pals,' I explained, all patience. 'You can't. They'll trample on you, break you up. Take an old man's word for it. I've been through a lot. I know what I'm talking about.'

And what did he say?

'They've pressed you down flat, they've smashed your spine, so all you do is croak.'

It was like a smack in the kisser. From my own son!

'You little squirt!' The blood rushed to my head. I nearly choked.

The daughter-in-law saw how things were and filled the glasses. We were by ourselves, the family, sitting round the table. The younger grandchild was asleep. The older one was still playing on the floor. Putting his trainset together. A clever toy, foreign. The train moved off. Stopped at the signal. Moved again.

It did me good to look at him. Good lads, my grand-children. I tried another tack.

'OK, suppose you're right. You say we mustn't let them get us down. You'll carry on, as before. Only underground. What about the kids? Don't you give a damn? You have obligations. A serious responsibility on your shoulders.'

The daughter-in-law butted in:

'If anything happens I'll look after things. I can manage. Don't you worry, dad.'

I took a look at her. Easy to say she could manage. Must

be joking. Since that illness, she's been half dead. Thin as a rake, always running a temperature. And where would the money be coming from? Come on, tell me! My son spoke before I could:

'If anything happens, you'll help, won't you dad?'

The cheek of it. They've learned to rely on their elders for material things. What a Sunday! They ask you to Sunday dinner and make a nervous wreck of you. I pulled myself together and clinked glasses with the boy. Man to man.

'I can understand you. But you're reaching for the moon. You should certainly wait a bit . . .'

'Oh, come off it, dad. You said the same before: "it'll come to nothing", "why not meet them half way?", "take what's on offer", "if you don't they'll crush you". But ten million people joined. That's a force to be reckoned with.'

Pigheaded, he is! Nothing gets through! If he'd only listened to his father and left the country when he had a chance. I wrote to my brother. He's been living in Hamburg for two years now. Doing well for himself. Promised to help. Poles get work permits, jobs, all sorts of good things showered on them nowadays, so my brother says.

The boy just laughed at me.

'Leave? Now? When we have a chance?'

'You've had your chance, you chump!'

That's how stubborn he is. Like a rock. Gets it from me. My dad used to lay about me at times. 'Won't do it again will you?' he would ask. 'Oh yes ' will,' said I. It's in the blood, in those damned genes of ours, or whatever they're called.

I pulled myself up once more and tried logic.

'I'm no coward. During the Occupation, my place was stuffed with underground papers. We kept them in the coal bunker. And in Stalin's time? Ask Kwiatkowski. The Security were after him and we kept him in our attic for a month! That's a fact. I could have got a long stretch for that!'

31

'That's ancient history, or maybe you made it all up,' the cheeky young devil replied. Smiled. Patronizing me! I noticed him wink at his wife. I felt helpless. And that vodka wasn't going down at all well. Had a nasty smell. Put me off. I looked at my fairhaired grandsons, and my heart bled for them. The younger kid looked like an angel, sleeping sweetly. What would become of them? Was there any future for them at all?

If only my daughter-in-law was a bit more down to earth. But she's just as much of a hothead. None of that womanly common sense. Birds of a feather, they are. We were still sitting at the table. The way they looked at me, I felt like an old rat who'd crawled out of his hole and would crawl right back in again. In our set-up even family life isn't normal. Nothing escapes their clutches.

I tried again.

'I've never hidden behind anybody's back. In our office, most of them stayed with the old union. I was one of the first to join Solidarity. The old man warned me – the manager, I mean – more than once that they wouldn't like it at head office. I didn't budge. Stuck to my guns.'

'That's nothing to boast about. What matters is sticking to your guns now.'

I was genuinely surprised.

'What is it you have in mind?' I asked.

No reply. He just got up, rummaged in the corner. Moved a plant pot with a palm in it, lifted the carpet, squatted down, and pulled a pile of papers out of a hole. Smoothed them out and started reading in a low voice. Bulletins issued by the underground Solidarity! Reports of strikes. Punitive actions. Solidarity activists rounded up and jailed. Walesa's appeal. One of the leaders had evaded capture and was carrying on in hiding.

'Don't keep that in the house!' I said, raising my voice this time. 'Take it out. Or destroy it! Right now!' I stretched out my hand for the papers. But he was quicker. Wouldn't let me touch them.

That was our Sunday dinner. Nerves, nerves, nerves. I had gone there to relax and enjoy young company. And instead I saw them sliding down the slippery slope. Two of a kind!

I'd had my fill of it. I got up, thanked the daughter-in-law.

'The food was tasty. You make those noodles just like his mother used to. Pity we don't speak the same language.'

They just nodded. The boy offered to walk home with me. I said nothing, but he came out with me.

We walked. In silence. There was nothing to say.

Out in the street I looked up at him and was flabbergasted. He was wearing one of those quilted coats, with a whole parade of badges. A medal of Our Lady, like the one Walesa always wore. A Solidarity badge. And others. It hurt my eyes to look at them. So bright, nobody could fail to notice them.

He straightened himself up.

'Sitting on your arse. This is the time to take them on!'

Thinks he's a knight crusader! Charging tanks with lances! But I kept my cool. Even pretended to yawn. Nothing I could say would change the obstinate wretch's mind. All I knew was that I had to send him home fast. If they saw that show on his lapel, he'd had it. He could be interned. They would search the flat. I preferred not to think about it.

Just then, I saw a patrol, not a hundred metres away. Four of them. I had to get rid of the young whippersnapper somehow.

'Here's my tram! Bye!'

I shook hands and ran to the stop. When I dared to look again, he had turned back. I relaxed. I walked on, slowly. The patrol came towards me. Militia, watchful eyes, stripped you naked. Maybe the vodka had worked at last. Or was it the sudden relief from tension? Anyway, the devil got into me.

'Good day, gentlemen,' I called out.

They stopped. So did I.

'What's the matter with you?' asked a militiaman.

'Nothing at all. I was just thinking, we shall come through this war all right.'

They closed in on me.

'Who's "we"?' asked one, with sideburns, his eyes shining angrily.

'Our people have come through a lot of things,' I said. 'I'm quite hardened myself. 2072 days I came through, and somehow I never gave up.'

'Why 2072?' The one with sideburns showed interest.

'That's how long the German Occupation lasted.'

The one with sideburns grinned crookedly.

'You don't say! Quite the mathematician, aren't you?'

They took me in for twenty-four hours. Kept me in a cellar for ten of them and the rest of the time I spent clearing snow off the streets. But I'd saved my boy. If he'd walked on with me they'd have pulled him in for sure.

The Horn of Plenty

———————*———————

Name is Kepka. S. Kepka. Pensioner. Retired. On account of ulcers. Two stomach operations.

I'd been looking quite a while for a part-time job. Nothing too hard. My papers are okay. I'm a party man. Served in the militia, just after the war. Wounded (in the calf, a flesh wound) in action against the underground. I haven't got much education, but I've done office work. In personnel. They wanted people they could be sure of. The people's power was only just finding its feet, and there were plenty of wolves in sheep's clothing around. We had to X-ray their papers. Find out all about them. I did the job conscientiously. Some tried to grease my palm but I wouldn't play. Anyway, that sort of thing could land you in the downstairs cells pretty quick. They chucked me out of personnel after October 1956. Lots of Security people were thrown out at the time. Even the captain I used to report to got the sack. I wangled a job as a storeman. I've stood by the system from the beginning. Never wavered once.

My mate at the warehouse said one day after a drink or two:

'You know what, Kepka. All Poland, from the Baltic to the Tatra mountains, from the Bug to the Oder, is one big concentration camp, and the prisons are like punishment cells in it, see?'

I saw red and reported the reactionary rat straight off. But vigilance isn't what it was. Nothing happened to him.

I'd had a bad stomach for years and it kept getting worse

all the time. I was pensioned off from the warehouse. I could make do but I started getting bored. A working man isn't used to so much spare time.

I pub-crawled for a bit, gambled, filled in lottery coupons. Then I put on my thinking cap and set about finding a part time place. I reported to our local party office, told them I was available. They wrote down my particulars and told me to wait. I waited and waited. I got a job at last, just a month before the war began. I work as a porter, three shifts a week, twelve hours a shift. In a beautiful high-rise. Only foreigners live there. A proper Tower of Babel, it is. All colours, from yellow to jet black. They speak their own lingos. You should hear tham jabber! Some speak Polish fluently enough, but there are words they simply can't pronounce. Conditions are good. I sit in the hall, in uniform, brown with green facings, and keep watch on the revolving glass doors. They have to go in and out that way. There's a box across the road with a militiaman always on duty. I'm in touch with him the whole time. You have to tread carefully and I've had special instructions. A tall, well-dressed civilian at the ministry told me how to work this beat. It was quite an important post, he said. The imperialists had recently stepped up their efforts to undermine our system. Their tentacles reached everywhere. Foreign money played an important part in all this.

'So you understand what your duties are, comrade?' he asked in conclusion.

I certainly did. I have a great hatred for reaction, and I took to that civilian. A man after my own heart.

First of all, I have to take note when any Pole visits the foreigners. Question him, find out who he is and who he's seeing. Politely of course. I have to remember his particulars and put it all down in a special little book and send in a report through the proper channels every week. I know what is expected of me. Never close my eyes for a minute, although it's warm there and I find myself nodding at times.

The ginger-haired Englishman on the seventh floor gets more visitors than anybody. 'Wide circle of acquaintance', I said in my report. Somebody calls every day. He has women in. Shameless hussies – selling their bodies for money! One of them stuck a dollar in my pocket once. She was drunk. The cleaner came downstairs just at that moment and saw it. So I refused the dollar. The cleaner also reports, sure thing. I bow to the Englishman, always. I bow to them all. Rise from my chair whenever a foreigner comes in sight. Even a black. Makes no difference. They smile, jabber away in their own lingo, slap me on the back and all that. The Japanese are the politest. I bow, they bow back. Very well behaved. Those from Thailand have good manners, too. So do some of the others.

But the Englishman looks down on me. Tall he is, wears a check jacket, never an overcoat, flies through the hall to his car. Very smart car, silver colour. And off he goes! Wonder if he's a spy of some sort? He's generous, though, I can't say he isn't. Gave me a tin of ham. 'Polish Ham' printed on the tin. And some tinned pineapple and one of his shirts, with a grease spot on the sleeve. I took it all. Presents are OK.

But I watch the red-headed snake, without letting him know it. I fetch his newspapers from the kiosk. He can read our papers.

The pay here is peanuts. But the perks are OK. Not a day passes without something. Take the Japanese. Gave me a gas lighter. Toyota, it says on it. One night the Thais and their women got back from a booze-up somewhere. The women in long dresses, the fellows in black jackets. They all tipped me. Five dollars – three bills and some change. That's real money. The dollar's worth seven hundred today. And round Christmas and the New Year I took home presents by the sackful. It's a Horn of Plenty, no less. My shift is the best: until 10 p.m. Because of the curfew they all have to be back before that. The night porter is green with envy. He doesn't take half as much.

I'm pretty pleased with the job. I smoke foreign fags, Dunhills and Marlboro and all those. I wet my whistle with Napoleon brandy or that American hooch that smells of bugs. I'm not complaining. The one thing I dearly wish I could do is get my hands on that red-headed Englishman. Catch him red-handed, of course. Spying or wrecking.

I sit in my easy chair, with my notebook on my knees, keeping an eye on the lift and the main entrance. My mind on the Englishman. I can just see the look on that bastard's face: 'Komm,' I say, and I beckon him with my finger. The Englishman is all of a tremble. He begs; tries to bribe me. Nothing doing. I grab him and escort him to the militia-man's box.

But I can tell the bastard knows I've got my eye on him.

The Enemy

---------------------------------- * ----------------------------------

She was interned and they protested. Whippersnappers. Running wild, these youngsters. Learnt it from the adults, with their brawling and striking and hell-raising. They organized an appeal. Pinned it to the notice board in the assembly room. Everybody signed. Long columns of names. The contents just what you would expect: offensive and inflammatory.

'We demand the release of our Polish teacher, Joanna Winnicka,' etc., etc. They served a copy on the headmaster. The school was like a beehive: a constant buzz during break about the teacher and the appeal. But times had changed. The school now had a military commissar.

Major Stachon. Ex-combatant, called back from the reserve. Took part in the 1944 campaign, from Russia to Warsaw, as a boy. Major Stachon wouldn't handle them with kid gloves, he was well known as a disciplinarian. Even in his civilian job he had expected military compliance from his subordinates. Truth to tell he hadn't been too fond of civilian life. It seemed to him chaotic, sloppy. Insubordination wherever you looked. He was fond of recollecting his days in the army and most of all the days of the proper war when the Second Army had forced the dykes of Pomerania, and he, Stachon, had got his baptism of fire.

At first, he felt ill at ease in the school. Military commissar! What was he supposed to do? Nanny the children? He didn't like the idea. But duty was duty.

He gave the upper forms a talk on martial law, in the gymnasium. Then repeated it for the lower forms.

He stood straight as a ramrod in full dress uniform with medal ribbons. His voice carried well and he didn't use the microphone. They listened. But he didn't like the look in their eyes. Or their faces. There was just no comparison with the soldiers Major Stachon had addressed in the past, by companies or by platoons. New recruits were particularly worthwhile material. With their shaven heads, their dutifully staring eyes, ready to answer questions in chorus. Yes sir or no sir, just as required. Most of all he liked making an entrance or an exit. The scraping of boots as a roomful of soldiers sprang to attention. Here it was very different. Whispering and laughter at the back. He lost the thread at least twice and if he hadn't known his stuff by heart he might easily have got lost altogether. He ended by ringing out the ritual final chord: 'Any questions?' In the past, when he had been talking to real soldiers, this had always been greeted with silence. He would then add, 'Everything clear?' to which the chorus replied, with one mighty voice, 'Yes, Sir.' But in the school gymnasium a skinny boy with a triangular face and indecently long hair rose from the front bench and asked in a strong, carrying voice, surprising in such an insignificant creature:

'Why has martial law been introduced at all?'

Major Stachon nearly choked. Surely, that's what he'd been explaining for a whole teaching period, all forty-five minutes of it. Was the boy exceptionally thick? He didn't look it. So it must be a vicious, cynical provocation? He gave the little wretch a devastating glance and asked:

'Is he acting the fool? Or doesn't he need to?'

This was an old and well-tried ploy. He expected a chorus of laughter. But it didn't come. Silence. Except for those whispers at the back. Heads down. Whispering to one another.

Major Stachon was sweating. His collar felt tight. He saved the situation by telling the impertinent youngster to study the subject from a recently-issued pamphlet on the state of war, obtainable at any news stand.

'You have three days to read it.' Major Stachon broke off this unpleasant exchange, collected his notes and left the platform.

He wasn't pleased with his own performance. It was a defeat of sorts. He had let the boy off too lightly. His authority was at stake. His momentary embarrassment might have been noticed. The boy's eyes had been calm and steady. The major remembered him well. Got his name from the school porter. He was on pretty good terms with the porter. An old soldier and an old soak, but he showed respect to a superior officer and kept the major fully informed on matters of interest to him. Major Stachon put the boy's name down in his notebook and asked hopefully:

'Parents mixed up in anything? Wrong class background?'

'Nothing like that,' said the porter. 'He only has his mother, she works in the cotton mill and she . . .'

'Never mind!' Major Stachon had no intention of letting the porter get too familiar. He spoke to him as officer to private. The porter liked it and sprang to attention every time he had anything to report.

Major Stachon repeated the name once and remembered it forever. He had been trained to memorize exactly the parts of a machine pistol and rattle off service regulations. Once in, information would never be dislodged.

'It's a difficult assignment,' he confided to his chum, a serving officer, over a bottle of Baltic Vodka.

The chum looked at him with compassion.

'Felek, you aren't losing your grip, are you?'

This chum, who worked in the chief political directorate, had brought Major Stachon back from retirement. The major promptly took hold of himself. The conversation made him realize that his new job was not at all trivial or marginal, but on the contrary, a highly responsible one.

'The younger generation, you know,' continued the political officer. 'Our people's future lies with them, after all . . .'

This new-found belief in the importance of his task finally dispelled the uncertainties of the early days, and although he was still rather put out by two smart young women teachers, and by the whispers and laughter during the break, which he unhesitatingly put down to jokes at his expense, he made up his mind to deal firmly with the so-called appeal. The whippersnappers were demanding the release of an internee! The highest authority had made a decision, and these kids had the effrontery to question it! That woman, Joanna Winnicka, must have been quite a troublemaker!

'The highest authority,' he murmured to himself, genuinely indignant.

He had met the general in person, once. Many years ago, during winter exercises. The general had inspected his regiment. Stachon had stood in front of his men. The general had passed close by. A hard man. He had stamped out drunkenness among officers, for one thing.

With this shining example in his heart, Major Stachon walked into the common room. He made a short, straight, soldierly speech to the assembled teachers. He stressed the serious shortcomings of political education in the school and the harm done by excessive fraternization between teachers and pupils.

'You can see the results for yourselves!' Major Stachon let his voice ring for a second, trying not to look in the direction of the two pretty young teachers sitting under a bust of the bard.

He was a widower. Felt it, occasionally. He tried to concentrate on the wall where the national arms were displayed.

But he couldn't help noticing those two luscious creatures. He managed to collect his thoughts, however, and ended in a brisk, manly fashion.

'We have to find the ringleaders and put an end to this provocation,' he said, and left the room with a spring in his step. He wondered what impression he had made on the two girls.

Next he summoned every form teacher in the school to the headmaster's study for a private talk.

One of the two pretty girls was a form teacher. She didn't mince her words.

'The kids are absolutely right. It shows their integrity, their feeling for truth and their need to see justice done. Mrs Winnicka is a superb teacher, the best in her subject this school has had for years!'

Major Stachon was stupefied. He had exerted his manly charm – all to no avail. Pretty face, high bosom, long legs. Very much his type. And here she was talking such foul nonsense.

Obviously, his new field was full of weeds, some of them pretending to be pretty flowers! The whole series of interviews was a failure. Every form teacher was downright evasive. The names of the ringleaders remained unknown. In the end, the porter came to the rescue. He buttonholed the major in the lavatory and said:

'Korczyk did more than anybody to get that appeal going.'

The same boy! The impertinent pupil shortly to be examined on the state of war pamphlet.

Major Stachon prepared himself very carefully for the interview. He decided to take the boy unawares after school, bump into him as if by accident. He took him to the headmaster's study. The head, he had to admit, was behaving better than the rest of the teaching staff. He was making an honest effort to help.

Major Stachon led the boy into the study. Sat behind the

desk. Concentrated on the papers in front of him. The boy stood, waiting. Major Stachon felt his presence, noted various telltale sounds with satisfaction. The shuffling from foot to foot, the squeak of a floorboard. The boy's breathing was uneven. Was he getting nervous already?

'Well?' Major Stachon lifted his head. Like a cat with a mouse in its claws, granting it just one more moment of vain hope. 'Have you learnt the lesson I set you?'

Korczyk nodded without a word.

A proud boy. Sharp nose, pale complexion, triangular face, hair long as a woman's. But he looked you straight in the eye.

'Good,' said Stachon. 'But let's leave it for the moment.' He had a copy of the appeal ready to wave in Korczyk's face. 'What is this?' he asked sharply.

'Our appeal,' answered Korczyk without hesitation.

'And your appeal wrote itself, I suppose?' asked Stachon innocently.

'Of course not,' Korczyk retorted. 'I and a few friends of mine drafted it. But it expresses the views of every pupil in the school.'

Major Stachon hadn't expected the first stage of the investigation to be quite so straightforward. One of the ringleaders in the bag already.

'You admit it, then?' he asked paternally.

Korczyk nodded again, without speaking.

'Can I take down this statement of yours, then? Will you sign it?' He pressed the top of his ballpoint and took several sheets of paper. He wrote with pedantic care the word 'Statement' at the top of the first sheet. He looked at the boy again. Was it really going to be that easy? Would it be all over in a matter of minutes? He had expected the enemy to play a more cunning game.

He stopped to think a minute. Further questions would have to be simple and apparently innocent. He envisaged

an investigation in three stages. First, find the authors of the
appeal. He already had one of them. What about the others?
Second stage: find out whether some other person had put
them up to it. Inspired them from behind the scenes. For
one second he thought about the pretty young teacher. He
only had to squeeze this young pup a bit, and he would
come out with the whole story.

'Right, my dear chap.' He smiled benevolently. 'Now
tell me, who was in it with you? Who were your accom-
plices?'

'I take full responsibility,' interrupted Korczyk loudly.
'You won't get any other name out of me.' He ended in a
high falsetto. Obviously his voice was breaking.

A brave lad!

A warm feeling stirred in Major Stachon for a split
second. Then he proceeded with the interrogation of this
dangerous firebrand. He looked hard at him, and no longer
saw an adolescent, a schoolboy, with a pale spotty face.

He saw – the enemy!

CPD

*

No! Cost of living bonuses won't save me. Sausage – 190 zloty a kilogramme, fatback – 100, shoulder bacon – 250! Curd cheese used to be 12, now it's 54, an increase of exactly 350%. And coal? I've got this large stove and it eats the stuff.

That's what I was thinking on the way home from work. If an American senator had popped up in front of me at that moment I'd have told him all about prices and bonuses. Let them all know!

I met Kaziek near the station. Hasn't changed a bit. Carrying a bag of some sort.

'Doing a bit of shopping,' he said.

I peered in. Some sort of salami, looked OK. Palm margarine. Two tins of sprats. Where had he got it all?

'I have my methods.' He was as pleased as anything.

We lit up. Stood on the corner talking. Then went off together.

I had a look at my shoe. The sole was nearly off! Lucky it was frosty. It would be a poor lookout in a thaw. I'd nailed it back on once before, and lagged it with wire. Held for a week. You can't buy shoes my size. Boats, I need. But even if I took a smaller size, there aren't any. I stood in a queue a few days back. By the time I got to the counter the only pairs left were all for dwarfs. If I'd had any sense I'd have bought a pair, and found somebody to swap with. Everybody does it: buys whatever is going and exchanges it.

Kaziek looked me over, slyly, once or twice. He could see I wasn't too pleased with life.

46

'What d'you say to a snifter?'

I exploded.

'I've used all my vodka coupons long ago!'

'There are places,' he said, smirking in that way he has.

I know what 'places' charge. But he went on tempting me.

'I know an old girl who only charges 1000 a bottle.'

'1000 is a lot of money.' Mentally I measured it against the latest price list.

'She's the cheapest in town,' explained Kaziek. 'Do you know what they charge in Bimberstrasse?'

'Bimberstrasse? Where's that?'

'Brzeska Street, to you, you mug. They ask 1500, more at night.'

I held out a bit longer.

'Not many can afford it then.'

'Look, I'll put down 500, you do the same, and we'll be well away,' said Kaziek. He gets a pension because of his health, but he makes a bit on the side.

'Are you on?' He watched me and waited.

I gave in. I can't keep up with all these price rises anyhow. Might as well drown my sorrows.

We went on. Through an old gateway. A prewar building. A yard, then another. He told me to wait. I'd given him my 500 and I was a bit worried.

'Don't look so bothered. There's no other way out.' Kaziek smiled.

I smoked a cigarette. He came back.

'We have to wait another quarter of an hour.'

'Why?'

'The old girl doesn't keep any stock. In case of a raid.'

Of course she didn't. Fifteen minutes passed. Kaziek went off again. Came right back with a bottle. Baltic Vodka.

'We can drink it standing, with a cigarette to help it down or', he thought for a bit, 'I know a nice place.'

Off we went. He took me to the Palace of Weddings.

'Are you off your head?'

He pushed me towards the door and in we went. Marble, chandeliers, people handing in sheepskin coats to the cloak-room attendant. Everybody carrying flowers. Three wedding parties waiting in a queue. The brides in white. A grand show. Just like a film. But why had he taken me there?

'I have a friend here,' said Kaziek.

He leant over the counter in the cloakroom and talked to the old chap there, a purple-faced little runt. The man nodded and let us in amongst the furs and sheepskins. Worth a fortune, a million or more, that stuff. He led us to the far end. Had a little cubbyhole there. You could get three people in easily. The old runt brought us a glass, and some sausage sandwiches of his own. Kaziek poured him half a glass for his hospitality. Well earned. He drank it in one, wiped his mouth and rushed back to the counter to collect more fur coats and sheepskins.

Kaziek and I got to work. A quarter of a glass, then a salami sandwich. Good sausage that cloakroom attendant had.

'A bloody yokel,' said Kaziek. 'Brings it from the village.'

He'd always been down on peasants. Couldn't stand them. Not since he had worked the bus station, conning suckers up from the country. I asked how he'd come to meet the cloakroom man. He put me off with a joke:

'I've been married three times. We ought to know each other by now.'

Gets around, Kaziek. Maybe he orders his meat from the runt's village?

The cloakroom attendant had vanished. Busy. Must be making a pile. People will always pay more on such occasions.

I was keen to find out how Kaziek managed to balance his family budget. His two kids by his second wife are still

48

on his hands. I only have to pay maintenance, and only for one. It's easier for a divorced bloke, except at meal times. A woman can always make something out of nothing. But Kaziek wasn't a bit worried.

'I even did all right during the Occupation. You remember, round the old station.'

I remembered all right. I had worked there myself as a bootblack.

We had enough vodka for one more round when the cloakroom attendant came in.

'Finish it off now, boys. My relief is taking over.'

'OK,' said Kaziek.

I drank mine from the glass, he took his share from the bottle. We thanked our friend and left the Palace of Weddings.

It had got dark. The frost was holding. I could tell by my ears. But we stopped for a moment.

'Did you know,' said Kaziek, 'CPD is back.'

'CPD? That's some sort of organization, isn't it? Congress of Polish Democrats? Don't tell me . . .'

Kaziek hooted with laughter.

'Not Congress, you mug! Cognac! Cognac Produced after Dusk, CPD.'

'Where do they make it?'

'Everywhere. A hose and two cans is all you need. Yeast is hard to get though. Next time we meet, come to my place and we'll drink cognac! Take care! See you!' And he ran for his tram.

I've known him so long. Never any different. Cocky. Made that way. One of the lucky ones.

I walked to the bus stop. Took the express. Didn't have to wait long. But it's a bit of a walk home from the express terminus. Through an empty plot, good place to get mugged. Teenagers work in gangs of three or four. Ask you for a cigarette. While you're getting your packet out, they knock you on the head. Pull your watch off, go through your pockets. They jumped my neighbour just when he'd drawn some of his savings. I covered that part of the route pretty smartly.

The stove was out. Not worth lighting it. I lay down on the bed, in my clothes. Wanted a cigarette, but fell asleep. The cold woke me up. I was frozen stiff. I got up, switched on the electric fire. I was parched. There hadn't been much vodka but it was thirsty stuff. I found some water in a can. There was ice on top. I slept again, for a long time. It was past curfew. I crept to the window. The fire station was all lit up. Two firemen on night duty. Helmets, axes in their hands, running round the square. Feeling the cold, must be. Not properly kitted out. Stamping their feet. Flinging their arms about. I thought I knew one of them, Kwiatek by name. Couldn't be sure in a poor light at that distance. As bad as guard duty in the army, I thought. The night was dead quiet and cold. My bladder was bursting. I didn't want to go out to the latrine. They might pinch me, on the way. So long after curfew. In front of my window there's this dead old tree. Last winter a small bird was perching in the branches, and a big fat black one pecked it to death.

Just the night for CPD!

I pissed in a bucket.

Little Sunshine

————————— * —————————

I got a job as an inspector with the State Newspaper Distribution Agency. It's something to do with the economic
reforms, I think. I go round the kiosks. There are twenty-
eight of them on my round. I have to see they don't waste
electricity. Everybody's doing it these days. It's the cold.
The mercury went down to fifteen below last night. So I had
a good round this morning. They were all warming themselves well beyond the permitted limit. I enjoy my work.
I'm my own master. No boss hurrying me up, nobody
checking on me. I take my own time. I have my eye on some
particular kiosk. Creep up on it from the rear. Or else pre-
tend to be a customer, walk to the counter bold as brass,
stick my head into the hatch and take in the scene. She has
a little sunshine heater to right and left and a convector at
the rear. That's the sort of thing they get up to. Out with
the badge.

'Inspection!'

The woman inside takes fright. It's mostly women who
run the kiosks. Her hands shake. It's my job to write out a
report detailing 'illicit sources of energy used', and all that.
It's all there on the form, I only have to fill it in. It's hard on
their pockets. The fine is deducted from their commission.
We go through the whole palaver. She begs, she cries, she
promises. I don't say much. Just the odd word. And so it
goes on. She's trying to find out where I stand. I'm doing
the same with her.

The older women use more extra heat than anybody.

It's their blood cooling down does it. But some of the younger ones also indulge. One of them kept her kiosk like a sauna, she had so much extra heat on! Four times the limit! Then there was one pigheaded bastard I caught twice. Two days running in fact.

The harvest was good today. I caught one old trout. Always unfriendly, she is, puts on airs, treats me like dirt. Today I was on top for a change. Like a child she was. I showed the old bitch no mercy. Wrote it all down. Let her pay.

Round Victory Square all the kiosks were over the limit. It's cold there, all that open space, draughty, the wind cuts like ice. Sitting in a kiosk there is like being in a wind tunnel. One woman gave me a packet of Extra Strong, filter tipped. You can't get them in the shops now. My favourite brand. Don't make me cough, like the others. She threw in a packet of razor blades.

The best-stocked kiosk is the one just outside the station! How does she do it? Got everything, she has. Must have something going with the suppliers. Made me a nice present. Cosmetics, toothpaste, soap, a packet of washing powder! The wife will be pleased.

I walked on, gathering the harvest as I went. Only half the round done, and a bagful already. You scratch my back, I scratch yours. I don't have to write everything down!

Time for a break. I walked into the Phoenix. They have beer there sometimes.

'Not a drop today,' said the pregnant barmaid.

'What would you say to a packet of washing powder, now?' I ask her. 'With baby due any time you ought to be getting a few things together.' Her eyes lit up at this. It was good powder. Not that Popular that leaves the clothes full of holes. She gave me two bottles from under the counter. I needed the reviver. The cold was bitter, the wind worse than ever. On with the harvest!

There's one I've never taken anything from. Never taken advantage of her infringements.

'Hello there, sunshine!' That's how I started chatting her up.

She looked scared out of her wits. Pulled at the flex, and out went her Sunshine heater. What a laugh!

Pretty little thing, not much over twenty, neat dresser.

I've dated her for Saturday. She'll be there, for sure. I've got her where I want her. Has to come, whether she wants to or not. Coffee, cakes, vino, and . . . well, one thing leads to another . . .

The Silver Bird

———————— * ————————

You couldn't call him backward. If anything he's too big for
his age. Tall, well set up, an athlete's chest. Looks much
more than his thirteen years. Eats like a horse. Difficult to
give him enough. You could say that his mental develop-
ment hasn't kept up with his physical growth. That is not
uncommon. It comes right in the end. It must come right.
In any case, he can read and write quite well. He has some
interests. For instance, the Second World War. The 1939
campaign. The battle of Bzura. I feed this interest of his. I
put the right books in his way. Just recently I gave him *The
Doctor Can't See You*, the memoirs of a man who was para-
chuted into Poland during the Occupation. I ask him
questions to see what he makes of it all. No, he hasn't got
much of a head for it. He remembered nothing about the
Fan unit which fought in Polesie. But he remembered in
detail how the special agents were trained in Scotland
before they were dropped into Poland. He remembered the
special knives they had, their shape and purpose.

'Knife.' He says it over and over again. He likes the
sound of English.

And how they had to walk over the mountains without
food except for some corn stuffed in their pockets.

A selective memory, you might say. This is his third year
in the same form. He's undisciplined too. A typical fault, of
course, with fast-growing teenagers. They like to go their
own way. Some say it's because he's a late child – born too
late, in fact. That's nonsense. True, his mother was thirty-

nine when he was born. It just turned out that way. But what of it? People get on my nerves with their medieval ideas.

We went to the airport together. A cousin was returning from Britain by charter flight. She must've gone off her head to come back just then! She had left in October with a study grant. Decided she couldn't bear staying away in view of the situation at home and came back before her grant expired. That I call a classic example of mental decrepitude.

So we went to the airport to welcome her home. The boy and I. At the airport the military were very much in evidence. Lots of tanks. Barriers. Crowds of soldiers. And of the others. At the same time, the place looked empty. No traffic. Deserted runways. All a bit depressing. The radar scanner was turning, and that was all.

The boy was interested in everything he saw. We went into the terminal. He tried to get over the barrier into the customs shed. I had quite a job to stop him. Had to explain that some places were OK but others were out of bounds. He calmed down at last and concentrated on the arrival and departure screens. He spelt out the words in English. People turned to look at us. He talks loudly and stammers a bit. Still, I understand him. The loudspeaker announced a charter flight from London.

We went outside towards the viewing platform. Not many people, perhaps twenty or so. Guards everywhere. Even on the platform. The plane came out of the clouds. It was breathtaking! Flew across like a silver bird. Lost height and landed on the runway. A neat, smooth touchdown. A TU 134. I was lost in wonder, I must admit.

At that moment the boy broke away from me. He is so strong, I reeled back. His face was radiant. He stretched out his arms towards the plane. He was shouting something. He too was fascinated by that thrilling sight. The speed, the height. Straight out of the clouds! The child was over-whelmed by it. He ran like a deer. No obstacle could stop him. Over a fence, out onto the tarmac. Still running. I was paralysed. Soldiers! On both sides, arms at the ready. They pounced on the boy. One had his finger on the trigger. They bellowed at him:

'Halt! Halt!'

The boy paid no attention. I scrambled after him. Over the fence, I suppose – I can't remember. I shouted to the soldiers:

'It's my son! He's only twelve! He's handicapped.'

I had to use the word. It worked. They lowered their guns. I slapped the boy's face and dragged him away. The soldiers helped.

There was a lot of unpleasantness to go through. They took us to the guardroom. The officer was very suspicious. He took our names. Questioned us. Drew up a report. Their eyes were like lasers. In the end they let us go.

Did he understand any of it? I'm damned if I know.

War, or no war, it's all the same to him!

The Vetting Session

———————————*———————————

Tymoteusz Bryk was called in first. Bryk signs his column 'Smog', in English. Sturdy body on a cavalryman's bow legs. Served in the Second Polish Corps. Fought at Monte Cassino. Got several decorations, one of them British. Writes historical pieces about the Second World War. Disagreements with the censor: frequent. Character: impulsive but stubborn. Drinks. Face florid, hair grey, battle-dress worn on all occasions.

Bryk was clearly drunk. He rolled into the room and fetched up in the centre, where an empty chair awaited the interviewee. Bryk spurned the chair, pushing it out of the way with his foot. His blue, somewhat glassy eyes flashed as he inspected the examining commissioners seated behind a long, baize-covered table.

From left to right sat representatives of the Ministry of the Interior, of the People's Army, the Regional Committee of the United Workers' Party and the Workers' Publishing Cooperative. At the end of the table sat an individual whose function remained undefined.

Tymoteusz Bryk's flashing eyes stared at the board. His face broadened into a smile. A round face, not unlike a ripe apple. He moved briskly towards the table, leant over it, supporting himself with both arms. The reek of recently-consumed alcohol spread through the room.

'What are you doing here, Henryk, old chum?' Bryk's right hand deftly grabbed the ear of the representative of the Publishing Cooperative. The victim drew back but

Tymoteusz Bryk wouldn't let go. He held the ear firmly between two fingers and even gave it a tug.

'Not a nice thing to be doing, is it, Henryk my boy? Not nice at all.'

The representative of the Publishing Cooperative (another old soak, as his face showed quite clearly), instead of dealing with this painful affront as it deserved, looked like a criminal caught red-handed and mumbled incoherently.

The chairman (a full colonel with a PhD, an imposing person who would obviously stand no nonsense) reddened with indignation and raised a broad, fat hand. Simultaneously Bryk, who had let go of his chum's ear, raised his hand in an identical gesture. Both hands hit the table simultaneously with a resounding bang.

'What do you think you're doing?' yelled the colonel.

'Nothing,' Bryk retorted cockily. 'Just letting you know where you can stick your vetting session!'

Bryk's voice was thin but penetrating. He turned round, stuck out his backside at the board, screeched 'Fuck off' in English and reeled out of the room, banging the door.

The board sat in silence for a minute or two.

'That old hooligan should go before a tribunal.' The major in plain clothes representing the ministry was the first to speak. He looked at the colonel, who was busy mopping his face with a handkerchief.

They didn't have time to analyse the incident in depth and reach the appropriate decision. The door opened again and the next interviewee slipped in as quietly as a mouse.

Wysilek, normally a most abstemious person, had drunk enough that day to make him look a wreck. He was slobbering, and the lapel of his jacket was covered with a revolting mess, perhaps the traces of a snack, perhaps something unthinkable. He hiccupped. Hiccupped again. And again. But he did his best to look polite and humble. He made a low bow to each member of the board in turn.

'Here, about this martial law,' he burst out, with a stupid grin. 'I heard about it three days before – 10 December. From somebody on the committee.'

The party representative sat up.

'Who was that?' He sounded irritated.

'Rysiek, his first name was, but I can't remember his surname.' Wysilek stopped tittering and looked sad. He gave a sniff. A dewdrop hung on the tip of his nose. Then suddenly he drew up his thin frame to its full height and let out a prepared speech:

'This is vile, vile and contemptible! If it wasn't for my wife and children . . .' A giant hiccup sent him reeling straight onto the table.

The chairman (the full colonel with a PhD) drew his chair back into safety. The others shielded their faces with their hands. Their luck held: Wysilek's tortured stomach released nothing. The colonel got hold of himself sufficiently to manage a look of loathing . . . this was not what he had expected of the creative intelligentsia.

'Get out,' he said sharply. 'We shall talk to you some other time.'

Wysilek stared at him blindly. He had something else to say.

'Get out,' repeated the colonel impatiently.

It finally dawned on Wysilek that the interview was at an end. He bowed low to the board and left the room, reeling even more uncontrollably than Bryk had.

'That old hooligan Bryk got him pissed,' remarked the major in plain clothes helpfully. He wrinkled his brow. He was obviously preparing an elaborate indictment against Bryk. The party representative opened a paper folder and examined some documents.

The representative of the Publishing Cooperative, still recovering from Bryk's insult, gave the chairman a quick, cringing glance.

'In my view . . .' He started uncertainly and came to a full stop.

Nina S. (Polish cookery and advice to the lovelorn) was next on the agenda. Nina knocked daintily and showed her sweet little face.

'Am I in the way?' she trilled.

'But of course not.' The colonel's gesture was gallant and hospitable.

There was a violent noise at the door, and Wysilek burst in, elbowing Nina aside.

'I've remembered,' he shouted triumphantly. 'His name was Kurczak, it was Rysiek Kurczak who told me about this war. Comrade Kurczak, that is!'

The party representative jotted something down. Kurczak's name no doubt. The colonel got rid of the zealot with a menacing growl.

'Do sit down, comrade,' he said, politely indicating the chair to Nina. Peace at last!

The colonel sighed with relief and smiled warmly. He glanced appreciatively at Nina's shapely, only slightly hairy legs and her high-heeled shoes.

Those shapely legs were, alas, unsteady. Nina S. was as drunk as the rest of them. She subsided into the chair with a clatter, managed a quick seductive smile and passed out.

The colonel was very near apoplexy.

'This is a farce!' he croaked, banging his fist on the table.

'Eh, eh?' cried Nina.

They voted to adjourn until the following day.

Wastepaper

———————— ✳ ————————

Water was seeping in from below. It might've been the door. I stuck some rubber along the bottom but still it came through. The floor may be going. On a rainy day puddles spread all over the floor.

Must take her to a garage. Let them have a look. Take her to Stas. He knows his stuff. I can't afford to have her off the road, not for long, anyhow. The bills are piling up.

The wife brought a lot of wastepaper home from the factory. Wants to line the shelves in the cellar. The damp has got in there as well. A pipe burst and it was two months before admin sent anybody.

It was just bits of paper to me. I took a quick look. News-sheet of the party committee where she works. Issued after this war began. I remembered the date. Couldn't be bothered to read it. Felt whacked after the day's work. Anyhow, what would it tell me that I didn't know already? Nothing.

In the morning, though, I had an idea. I covered the floor with that paper, and chucked some more of it in the boot. When the first lot got wet I could replace it with dry sheets.

Then it all started. On Monday. Bad luck right at the beginning. We cabbies are superstitious about these things. The first fare wanted to go to Zawisza Square. There are four checkpoints on the way.

The fare was so keen to get there, I felt pretty sure he'd tip me. They halted us at the second checkpoint. Pounced on the car. Like dogs let off the leash. All because a piece of paper was sticking out. I hadn't tucked it in neatly under the front passenger seat, and half of a bulletin was shut in the door. The printed word hit them in the eye, and they stopped us. Told me to get out. Made me stand against a wall, hauled the passenger out as well. Two of them jumped inside and the hunt was on. They dragged pages of news-sheet from under the floormats, opened the boot and got out the spare paper.

'Underground stuff,' said one, turning the wet sheets this way and that.

'Have another look,' I said. 'Do you call this underground stuff?'

'Hostile propaganda.' He wasn't going to listen, he was too pleased with his catch.

I showed him a page. It said in large letters 'News-sheet of the Works Committee of the Polish United Workers' Party.'

'Can't you see?' I pleaded.

'We know those tricks. There are all sorts of ways of camouflaging the stuff.'

I took a look. Right on the first page there was an article about 'The role of the party in the new political situation.'

'See for yourself!' said I.

He called the other one.

'Something fishy here.' He spat on the ground.

'Very cunning,' agreed his mate. How could I explain? I turned the pages and found the headline I needed.

'Put an end to the anti-socialist diversionist provocation of Solidarity.' With three exclamation marks. Bold type throughout.

'There you are, you see.'

It went on for another half hour, this stupid game. I was slowly winning. Then they found, at the bottom of the first page, 'For internal circulation only.'

' "Internal" means to be kept in the works, so you shouldn't be hawking the stuff round the streets. Am I right?'

That was one I couldn't explain away. They seized all the paper. Took my particulars. And the passenger's. The passenger went raving mad. He had taken a taxi because he was in a hurry. They let us go in the end. My first fare! The whole day will be rotten, as likely as not. One thing is for sure. I won't touch any more wastepaper with a ten-foot pole.

It's poison!

The Peacock

———————————— ✳ ————————————

The station was nearly empty. Not many windows were open in the booking office, and the clerks sat there with nothing to do. A handful of travellers scattered around on benches or propped against walls. Some dozed, some stared into space. A few youths watched the flickering image on the television screen. The place was silent, dead. No frenzied rush, no push for tickets, no arguments, no entreaties, no queries about train times. The bums of both sexes who are part and parcel of station life, the boozy women of uncertain age, the cretinous tousle-headed males had vanished almost completely. A few such figures lurked perhaps in the darkest corners. Dreading discovery by the all-seeing eye.

The hush was deafening. Then a sudden clutter of nailed boots made a few passengers sit up. A militia patrol was crossing the empty concourse. Five large, well-fed men. They examined their surroundings. Woke up an elderly traveller to check his documents.

People kept their heads down. They tried to escape the sharp eyes of the militiamen. The patrol reached the steps leading down to the platforms.

Another burst of sound filled all that silent space, drowning the racket of the patrol.

People looked up again. And gaped in wonder. A large case on wheels rolled through the automatic doors. Huge, yellow, with metal fittings. Covered with colourful stickers advertising hotels and travel agencies in many languages.

It rolled for a few yards, stopped. Its owner followed, resplendent, clad in white sheepskin from head to foot, black himself, his hands glittering with gold rings. He strolled casually after the case, and gave it another powerful push with his long foot. It rushed forward on its little wheels, with a rattling, grating noise.

The patrol, ready to march down the stairs, stopped in their tracks. They looked round, staring intently, scowling, hands on their Kalashnikovs.

The black man and his luggage reached the middle of the concourse. A final kick with a soft, elegant, high-heeled shoe. The white coat disclosed a scarlet sweater over black velvet trousers. A peacock! The embodiment of freedom, exuberant, defiant. A freedom that can never be curbed.

People watched enraptured. Far distant lands, lights of trains disappearing into the unknown. That's what they saw.

A very small girl pointed, with a look of enchantment on her face.

'Mama, look, a black man!'

The mother angrily seized the little girl's hand.

But she too stared greedily at that proud and brilliant vision.

Gorgio [1]

————————————— * —————————————

The gypsy was dead drunk. Stood in the middle of the road, making a speech. He was an old gypsy, he said, a hardworking gypsy. And he wouldn't go a step further. He was done in. He dropped his double bass to the ground and demanded a taxi.

'Where can I get you a taxi!' The soldier on point duty sounded helpless. He looked around. Not a single moving light as far as the eye could see.

The gypsy pulled up a trouser leg to show a thick, hairy calf.

'These legs have packed up,' he nearly sobbed, shook his fist at the empty darkness and kicked at the case which held his instrument.

'Fuck it all!' said the gypsy, taking from his overcoat pocket a bunch of creased notes, some matches and a gaudy packet of foreign cigarettes. He made as if to trample them into the mud.

The soldier adjusted his Kalashnikov, knelt down, and collected the notes, the cigarettes and the matches. Pushed them all back into the gypsy's pocket. The gypsy stood up unsteadily and groaned.

The regular tramp of military boots was coming closer. The soldier stirred uneasily and moved the Kalashnikov quickly to the correct position.

'Now go away,' he begged.

The gypsy listened to the approaching patrol.

[1] Gorgio is a Romany word for a 'stranger' – a non-gypsy.

With a sudden access of energy he lifted up his instrument, swung it over his shoulder and stepped lightly off the roadway.

'You're a good bloke, Gorgio!' he called out to the soldier and pushed a packet of foreign cigarettes into his hand.

'Gorgio?' The soldier repeated the unknown gypsy word.

The Confidential Call

—————————*—————————

A depression. The weather was getting us all down. The Rio bar was closed. Where could we go? Couldn't even stand on a street corner. They latched on to you straightaway. At home, there were moaning parents: 'What's going to happen next? What ever will become of us all?'

We saw, without much emotion, Basil lumbering towards us. Breathing hard. Like an excited young elephant.

'Know what, lads?' he called out, 'They've been questioning the caretaker.' That in itself didn't do much for us. Lots of people were being questioned. But then it began to look a bit more interesting, even in Basil's disorganized telling. They were looking for Solidarity people. Bujak was mentioned. Also Janas.

Basil swore by all that's holy in this materialistic age that a man in plain clothes had been showing photos to the caretaker. The caretaker had looked through them, blinking sagaciously.

'If I clap eyes on them . . . I'll report them straightaway of course.'

The caretaker was a nasty. He would report all right. He had no time for us, and we had less for him. Our sophisticated utterances put him off. He lost his cool easily. We were still standing outside the closed bar. But things weren't what they had been a minute earlier.

Basil's story stimulated the imagination. Like the touch of a needle. Had we, in fact, seen any strangers? Anyone looking as if he were on the run? We hadn't, we thought.

The estate is a quiet backwater, tenants mostly white-collar workers. Small blocks round quadrangles. But we couldn't stop thinking about it. And we had all the time in the world to think. Time itself had slowed down. All higher educational institutions were still closed. No good thinking about the future. Couldn't be more bleak. The Independent Students' Union had been dissolved, and they were bound to pull in some of us. A grim prospect all round. In the evening we played our usual guessing game: which snout would we see tonight on the box? Which of the scum would come up with a new eulogy on the state of war and the happy future in front of us? What rhetorical tricks would he use? Would he try to dodge the dangerous reefs or bash away regardless? Would the programme turn out to be an outlet for personal grudges? Or the lament of a sage saddened by events? You could go on *ad infinitum.* The snouts were well matched. Natural selection. A march past of pigs.

'Crooks on parade,' said Wladek.

For decorative purposes add a few sclerotic elders, probably unaware of what it was all about and how they were being used. They were merely pitiful. As Wladek put it, 'This has finished the grandfather myth for me.' It was a family thing, this. Wladek's father never stopped telling him stories about his grandfather. Grandfather had been the family idol.

But to return to the snouts. Our masochistic evening rites produced an idea of sorts. The concept came from Baby, a shy, thin, only child, full of sexual hang-ups. Brought up by doting parents in a hothouse atmosphere, he provided the rest of us with a considerable amount of amusement.

Anyway, it was Baby who reminded us that one of the snouts lived on our own estate. True, we hadn't seen him for over a week. Maybe he had decided to avoid contact with the people. Or perhaps, closeted in his study, he was about to create a masterpiece, inspired by the new era.

'Can't have been given a villa yet?' asked someone.

'No, it doesn't work that fast. Not in this country.'

Our doubts were soon settled: Rysio had seen him the night before. Walking his dog. A griffon, answers to the name of Koko.

We worked on Baby's idea. The snout was a supersnout. Writer by profession. On the telly, he came very near the top. Highly valued, obviously. We remembered his performances well. In real life we hardly noticed him. Squat little man. Briefcase, sheepskin coat, fox-fur hat. Wrote novels we no longer read. Our literary taste was fairly sophisticated. We liked our literature to be literature, we were into things like *The Language Preserved*, and not just because the author had got a Nobel Prize. We had discovered *Auto-da-fé* for ourselves a long time ago. So of course the works of our neighbour on the estate didn't qualify. Kitsch, sexual tackiness and vulgar machismo went together, in his writing, with a preconceived and false picture of reality. Truth was to be found only at our end of Europe, and to declare yourself for the East was a heroic decision. He discreetly wrapped the East in a veil of mystery. He hinted that Moscow was the Third Rome, and that we had shared the same cradle. True humanism, of course, was the monopoly of the East. This was the sum of supersnout's vision, his historical and moral philosophy. His work clearly wasn't worthy of our attention. A waste of time. For years, his books had been published in vast editions, through all the changes and upheavals. They were on display everywhere, from the windows of booksellers to the apartments of the new intelligentsia, where they adorned the shelves of room dividers. They were a constant, they were inescapable. We had grown up in his shadow: he had deprived us of the light we needed. We realized the danger early on, and did not drown in that sticky claptrap, replete with descriptions of nature, food, and horse sweat, laced with love of God and Poland. That was it: his phoney patriotism and Catholicism were the ultimate obscenity. His television appearances had been, of late, crammed with religious and patriotic platitudes. His face had acquired, over the years, a cast of such hypocrisy that he could stand in for the wolf, dressed up as Red Riding Hood but unable to stop his mouth watering.

We let ourselves go, each adding his own embellishment to the composite portrait of our neighbour. Day in, day out, we had to suffer the wormeaten grandiloquence of his kind with no opportunity to reply. We rubbed our hands. But not because we were cold. We felt the excitement of the chase. The hounds would soon be drawing the covert . . .

It needed careful planning. Arkadiusz took care of that. His mind is cool, precise, not subject to facile emotions. Why is he reading oriental languages? He's a born mathematician. For entertainment, he reads Wittgenstein and often embellishes his conversation with that philosopher's aphorisms. Truth to tell, he has no worthy partner among us. But he is used to running with the herd, and sticks to his contemporaries.

'I've got it,' Arkadiusz drawled. Our curiosity was white hot. 'We must telephone the militia this very day and give them the address of a flat where someone resembling Bujak, or Janas, is hiding.'

We liked this. We liked it very much. We savoured this tasty morsel in appreciative silence.

'Better say Bujak,' Arkadiusz decided. 'He's first-class bait and ought to get a bite.'

We sprang into action. Long Michael was entrusted with the preliminary recce. He came back full of joy.

'Working in his study. I heard the typewriter.'

We decided that the afternoon would be best. People

would be coming back from work. The winter dusk sets in early. But visibility wouldn't be too bad: we wanted to see the show.

Arkadiusz christened the game 'The Confidential Call'. There was an argument as to how the informer should introduce himself. 'Well-wisher'? 'Right-thinking observer'? 'Right-thinking' sounds absurd, and artificial. Whoever uses such adjectives nowadays? Only the newspapers. We were about to opt for 'well-wisher' when Arkadiusz spoke up again:

'Far-fetched. Sounds too melodramatic. We have to build on reality. It makes for credibility. Let's make him the caretaker or house manager. It will sound natural. And it will make the game more predictable and easier to play.'

He persuaded us easily. Logic and realism. We had no scruples about the caretaker. We had seen him entertain the militia on many occasions, and not only with bread and salt. His guests came out reeling, swollen with vodka. And then, there was that brother-in-law of his. 'My brother-in-law has gone to London.' 'My brother-in-law is in Sweden.' A murky character. Turned up sometimes in a big Russian car, hooting for the caretaker. The caretaker and his family would dash out to greet him. No, we had no scruples. Let the caretaker do the telephoning. Bolek volunteered to play the part. The caretaker has a hoarse voice, words come out in a rush. We improvised a rehearsal. Bolek was magnificent. A solid, reliable informer.

The time dividing us from zero hour flashed by. Lunch at home, mentally absent, a mooch around, a look at a book, and we were off.

We chose a telephone box close to the supermarket. Bolek went in. Arkadiusz was with him to direct his performance. We posted a guard at the corner and agreed the signal.

Our quarry lives in complex F, block three. We placed

ourselves in the building opposite, at the window on the fourth landing. Visibility left nothing to be desired. We could see Bolek in the phone box. He lifted the receiver. Dialled a number . . .

What follows is the story as told by Arkadiusz when it was over. I have no doubts about the precision and accuracy of his report.

'Duty officer, please. Caretaker of complex F, Skarpa Estate. I've seen him in block 15/17, Rzodkiewki Street, flat number 44, third floor. Yes, yes. I saw him with my own eyes. He walked in, looked around. Had his collar up. Ran upstairs to the third floor. Who?! What do you mean, who? Bujak, of course, Zbigniew Bujak, Solidarity. Yes, yes. How? Because, this morning, a plain-clothes man from HQ showed me his picture. Yes! Identical! I'll wait. No, he hasn't left. Of course. The Skarpa Estate, Rzodkiewki Street, block 15/17, flat 44. I'll be here.' Bolek put the receiver down.

Bolek and Arkadiusz joined us at the observation point.

'They took the report seriously. Got more worked up by the minute. They'll be here any time now.'

It was getting exciting. Brought back memories of films. American thrillers. City jungle. New York. San Francisco. Drug pushers' hang-outs. A stool pigeon tells all . . . Squad cars rush through the streets.

We waited. It didn't take long.

'They're coming!' Our lookout in the shape of Wladek took a handkerchief out of his pocket. He waved it in a ladylike way.

Two radio cars. Followed by the meat wagon. Plain-clothes men poured out of the radio cars. Uniformed men out of the wagon. They were quick and efficient. The civilians, burly, lightfooted men in quilted jackets, ran into the courtyard of complex F. Militia took up position on the perimeter. The civilians divided into three groups and ran towards the three staircases of block 15/17. We concentrated on the middle staircase. Only one civilian remained outside, the rest disappeared.

Alas, we were unable to follow developments indoors. What did they do? How did the eminent writer conduct himself? We had to put our imagination to work: they must have rushed in, split up between different rooms. The writer, absorbed in creative activity, may not have heard the bell. So they force the door. Push past the writer's wife. Look in the bathroom, in the loo. Throw clothes out of the wardrobe. Check the entresol. We knew the plan of the flat. Baby's parents occupied an identical one. The writer is motionless for a moment, overcome, numbed. Then rouses himself: 'You have no right! What is this supposed to mean?' 'Shut up, you, or . . .' They put him against the wall and search him thoroughly.

We waited for fifteen minutes, perhaps longer. The door downstairs banged. They were back in the courtyard now. They had brought him with them. No overcoat. Two of them held him by the arms. It looked as if he was trying to resist. They dragged him along. We couldn't see his face. It was getting dark. There were more and more people in the yard. And at the windows. The caretaker hadn't turned up yet. Visiting his beloved brother-in-law perhaps? Good for us. Let the spectacle unfold, let it go on as long as possible. The cordon of militia round the flats was like a wall. A menacing wall. Then, a Fiat drove up in front. Two civilians got out, carrying their bulk with dignity.

'Staff officers,' whispered Arkadiusz. The plain-clothes men dragged the writer towards the bosses, let go of him. The writer searched feverishly through his pockets. Found what he wanted. Showed it to them. They read attentively. Looked at him again. Lightning change of situation: handshakes, smiles, more handshakes. The plain-clothes men withdrew into the background, heads bowed. The writer was left with the bosses. Lively exchanges. Further hand-shaking. Nearly an embrace. Action completed. No Bujak. The radio cars drive sadly away. And the wagon. The bosses' Fiat brings up the rear. The bosses are still waving to the writer. Bye! Bye! The writer stands alone. It was very uncomfortable for him. At this juncture, the famous writer obviously didn't know how to get home. The court-yard was full of people. The squat figure shrank further, the head drooped. He went back inside like a dog with its tail between its legs, trotting comically on his short legs. Stumbled where children had been sliding near the dust-bins. Barely kept his balance. With a final effort, he vanished into his staircase.

Only then did the caretaker emerge from his hole. Looking lost.

'What's going on? Whatever has happened?'

He sounded desperate.

Madam Amalia Bessarabo

———————— * ————————

Amalia Bessarabo was a woman of some bulk, yet her move-ments seemed light and graceful. Her eyes, black and very large, were her most notable feature. For years she had been plying her trade through the outer suburbs. A short, stout woman inseparable from an old-fashioned case containing the necessary instruments. Men in little single-storey houses and old tenements automatically associated her short, plump person with their own womenfolk. They greeted her with respect. Madam Amalia was a midwife, and highly thought of. People often rang her up in the middle of the night and she never said no when she was needed. In the obstetric hospital where she was employed, her remarkable gentleness brought peace to women writh-ing in pain. When all was over she would hold up a red wrinkled infant and announce in her ringing contralto:

'There's a bonny boy, sound as a turnip!' Or, 'It's a girl!'

There were traces of some dialect from further east in her speech, but they were not often noticeable. No-one knew anything for certain about her history. When not at work, she would settle herself down to read the cards. Just at the moment, in these hard winter days, she concentrated on her cards more than ever. They provided a magical world, the only credible world of signs and prophesies. She read them like a book. Lately its pages had been black with ill omens. To get away, she rushed about on shopping expeditions, covered a large area of the city, talked to sales people in markets, stores, and bazaars. She knew exactly what was obtainable, sensed intuitively what was about to appear in a shop somewhere. She returned from those expeditions laden with bags and packages. For some time afterwards we could hear noises from her flat: clatter, rattle, gurgle, rustle. She was unpacking her purchases. The kitchen, the loft, the cupboards in her room, and the bathroom were soon full of them.

Sorting out her spoils in the cramped flat – boxes of tea and coffee, sacks of cereals, flour and sugar, tins of preserves and pickles, jars of jam, butter, margarine, bottles of vinegar, oil, vodka and spirit, cartons of cigarettes and matches, boxes of washing powder, tubes of cream, tablecloths, towels, rolls of wire, peasant dolls, reams of writing paper, rolls of toilet paper – Madam Amalia would occasionally break off, straighten her ample form, dry the sweat off her face, take a quick look at the mirror, tidy the dyed locks on her forehead, and, finally, glance at the portrait above her widow's couch. The man in the painting was large and majestic, with a drooping moustache and wearing an unidentifiable uniform. Madam Amalia would sigh a little, cross herself and return to the heavy task of stacking away her purchases. Her stocks grew at such a rate that things began to go off. They gave off bad smells, they fermented, they swelled up, and a thorough inspection became necessary every few days. Some things she salvaged by boiling. She skimmed layers of mould from jars. She had little time left for setting out the cards. In the evenings she took the telephone off the hook. She no longer had any desire to go out visiting pregnant women. Yet only a short time ago she had been so delighted by the arrival of every new human being!

'They breed like rabbits,' she said brutally.

She sat at the green table following avidly the mysterious prophesies of the cards. The future never looked anything but bleak. Late at night, in her dressing gown, with her hair

77

down, she gazed out into the blackness and sighed as she did when she glanced at the big man in the picture. She looked like a witch. She slept badly and moaned in her sleep. She asked no-one in to her flat except a young neighbour, a girl student newly arrived from the provinces to live with her grandparents. She invited the girl once a week, served coffee in beautiful china cups, and talked.

Another world, long dead and buried, emerged from her stories. A Romania which no longer existed. A Lvov which was no more. The Orient Express. The salons of *haute couture*. Her own christening, by Archbishop Teodorowicz. A morocco-bound album full of yellowed photographs came out of the drawer. An old man with a beard and a bonneted matron. They were her parents, and their world was even more remote. Kishinev. Her grandfather murdered in the Kishinev pogrom. Odessa. The Richelieu statue. A pleasure boat, Greeks, Turks. A Turk in a fez, smoking a hookah. Melons full of sun.

She would break off unexpectedly, cross her thick fingers decked with rings and stare straight ahead in silence.

Today, Madam Amalia told the story of the dangers which had almost engulfed her in her time. Three times people had tried to take her life.

The first time was during the Kishinev pogrom. She had hidden under the bed.

'But, Madam Amalia,' wondered the girl, 'that can't be right! How old would it make you?'

Madam Amalia dismissed this with a wave of the hand and continued.

The second incident had occurred during the revolution. Her beauty had saved her then. And the third time, during the Second World War, she had bought her life with gold.

She broke off again, stared ahead, then came to.

'I'm sorry for you!' She looked kindly at the young student.

78

The girl was slim, raven-haired, dark-skinned. Perhaps not unlike the young Amalia of long ago. She patted the girl's cheek.

The girl felt ill at ease in the supercharged air of old memories and haunting sorrow. She wished to return to the real world. Her eyes moved quickly over the stacks of provisions piled up on shelves, on the couch and in every corner.

'It's like a warehouse! What do you want with it all?'

Amalia's black deep eyes were filled with anger.

'Silly little girl!'

She caressed a parcel close to her. A powdery mess fell out on the floor. The evening continued. The two women sieved flour and barley. Little black worms had set up home in the sacks.

'Fuck the thieving bastards,' said Amalia Bessarabo in Russian.

The Distributor

———————————— * ————————————

Every time I had to carry the stuff on me, I took the kid.
Marysia was quite pleased with the arrangement. This way,
she said, she had more time for herself. As a caring mum,
she warned me to watch out. I did, of course. The kid loved
it all. Expeditions with dad were just the ticket. I remember
how I loved Saturday outings with my dad. There was
more variety in our expeditions, the kid's and mine. We
went all over the city. The demand for our paper was growing all the time.

We used to take a tram from Ochota to Grochow, then
change to a bus. The landscape changed. End of the urban
sprawl.

'Look – snow on the trees!' The boy clapped his hands.
'It's pretty!'

Some days we took the electric train. Fields, cows. The
child even spotted some thatched cottages. Just like going
on holiday.

Looking at it another way, he provided valuable camouflage. Who would bother about a father in charge of a four-
year-old? A rucksack or bag was no problem, either. A dad
collecting his kid from kindergarten, getting some shopping
done on the way. After all, that's how most young married
couples live. That was my line of reasoning. Touch wood,
I've been proved right. We had no accidents. The kid was
my shield, and he benefitted too. He got to know a lot about
people and life. He was interested in all we saw. He learnt
to recognize the makes of cars, and could beat me at it. He

knew the important buildings: Forum, Rotunda, the churches. If we happened to be in a remote suburb at dusk he would look back to see the light on the Palace of Culture. It was a beacon for him. That amused me. When I was his age the palace seemed to me an ugly monstrosity not worth thinking about. The kid learnt about directions, distances. Became an expert on the topography of the city. He knew his way round labyrinthine new estates better than I did. He was my guide sometimes. We had some odd experiences. Once two drunks rolled past us, one of them saying over and over again in a tearful voice:

'Life's cord is getting thinner.'

'What?' asked the kid.

I explained the metaphor in some detail. He remembered and often, later, used it in most unexpected circumstances.

We had been at it for a month. We both liked it. The only thing to make me apprehensive was his reaction to people in uniforms. He could tell which was a railwayman, a tram driver, a guard, a soldier or a militiaman. Never failed to sort out the militia from the army, though their present uniforms and the four-cornered caps they wear are nearly identical. I once asked how he managed to tell them apart.

'By their scarves,' was the instant reply.

He can't stand the militia. Reacts immediately with a hostile look.

'Why are they militiamen?' he often asks. It is a difficult question to answer.

He decided to find out for himself. He was going to ask a man on traffic duty. I managed to dissuade him, with some difficulty. His alertness really knocked me back. Once he pointed to a man in plain clothes shadowing us.

'He walks like one of them.'

'Like who?' I asked.

'A Ubek, a Security man.'

Surprise. But it shouldn't have been. The night martial

law was proclaimed, they came to our flat. A general search. Tore everything apart. Came again a week later. Took me away, for forty-eight hours. Traumatic experience for the kid. Could easily have developed into a psychosis. There was that risk, of course, but I didn't think too much about it. My concern was the stuff and getting it to the right address. What we called 'the delivery point' in the new jargon of conspiracy. I was rather proud of being one of the few distributors with a clean slate: no accidents. Born under a lucky star, said the guys at the printers. True enough. But to a large extent it was the boy. At times I felt relaxed and lighthearted as though we really were just out for a walk. Spring was breaking out. Blue sky, sunshine. We walked slowly, staring at the birds. There were thousands of them sitting on the rubbish heaps. Crows and jackdaws. It kept my nerves steady. I almost forgot about the stuff in the bag. There have been some longish sentences lately. Two years, a year and a half. Heniek, for instance, copped it. Silly business, that. Somebody pushed him, in a crowd. Heniek: 'You could say sorry!' It developed into a row. The other bloke reported him to the nearest patrol.

Then there was poor Bozenka. I'm scared of prison, I admit. But the kid helped me to shake off these gloomy thoughts.

Once, just once, I had a real scare. We were on the tram. It was packed although it was past the rush hour. The boy took note of everything around us, as usual. The plastic on the back of the seat had been torn.

'Look!' He touched my arm.

I nodded without paying attention. Then the kid, quite loud:

'The Ubeks spoilt it looking for something.'

Four years old and so sure of himself. The kid connects. I felt quite panicky. My hands started sweating. You meet all sorts of people in a tram. Ubeks in plain clothes, militia, informers, or just plain fools. There could easily be trouble. Somebody might ask me for my identity card, stop the tram, call a patrol. I was carrying a sackful of the stuff. A few hundred of the *War Weekly*. Fresh, still smelling of printer's ink. A fine sight I should look! But the people were solid this time. No black sheep. The driver smiled broadly, the others did too. A general look of approval. He loved it. Pushed his finger deeper into the tear.

We reached our destination. Safely.

Silent Night, Holy Night

──────────── * ────────────

The city dies early in the evening. Buses move like ghosts, the last passengers crouch nervously inside them. Few streetlights are lit. The streets are dark yawning holes. Restaurants and cafés are closed, in mourning. The legs of chairs upturned on tables proclaim it. And the nickel glint of an idle espresso machine. The empty shelves.

The city sinks into the boredom of night-by-order. Some dog-owners may still be seen with their four-legged companions. They stick close to the buildings and keep one eye on their watches.

The silence is almost unbroken. A sound, when it comes, reverberates from wall to wall. People creep to their windows, draw the curtains open and look out. Not asleep after all. They are keeping a vigil.

There have been more than a hundred evenings like this since the war started.

A church clock struck eleven. At the last stroke, a dim figure materialized from around the corner. Crept along, clinging to the wall. A belated pedestrian. Would they catch up with him?

That was what the elderly woman looking out from the window on the first floor must have been wondering. The sky was moonless, starless. Loud steps suddenly rang out in the silence. People at the windows saw a group of soldiers walking in the middle of the road. It wasn't a patrol. There were four of them, straggling along. They had taken their belts off and were waving them about wildly. The buckles struck sparks from the flagstones. The soldiers walked un-steadily, jostling one another. Then they stopped to listen to the cats' serenade coming from the park.

'Puss, puss,' the soldiers chanted.

The cats screeched in terrifyingly human voices.

The soldiers noticed the figures in the windows. They took their caps off. Threw them in the air. The caps fell on the road. They sank unsteadily to their knees, trying to retrieve them.

'There's only one Poland,' shouted one of them, and reeled into a lamp-post. He bowed solemnly to the shadows in the windows and embraced the lamp-post, his head sagging on to his chest. Then he staggered after his friends.

They were now close to the crossroads. A bus on its way to the garage came by. Halted to let the soldiers pass. But they stopped again and performed a curious drunken dance.

The soldier who had yelled out before cursed horribly. He threw his cap onto the roadway and trampled it under-foot. The others encouraged him with inarticulate howls.

The voices and the stamping of nailed boots hung on the silence for a time.

The people in the windows drew their curtains and turned off their lights. One dim silhouette could still be seen in a small attic window.

The Spring Walk

——————————*——————————

Some days are worse than others. Everything, but everything, turns into a nightmare. Alas, the bad days are more frequent. Today happens to have been very bad indeed. And very long. I came home like a wet rag. Maria never asks unnecessary questions. She senses my mood straightaway. The food was ready, we sat down. She'd managed to buy some offal and tried to turn it into a Hungarian goulash of sorts. When I started eating, it was tasty enough, quite spicy. But what a stink! I flew off the handle. And to think that that moron Franek bought half a pig in his village; all that finger-licking grub to himself! 'Prewar production,' he called it. He brought some to eat at the office, sausage, black pudding, the lot. Didn't treat anybody else, of course. Maybe the goulash wasn't as high as all that. But in my state of mind today it was all I needed. I pushed the plate away. Making a bit of a noise about it. Maria looked at me, scared. I got hold of myself. It was quite an effort.

'I don't feel like eating.' I squeezed the words out of myself, and lit up. I smoke Caros. They weren't too bad to start with, but they're revolting now. They're harsh, they give you a sore throat, they're more like chaff than tobacco. Everything is turning foul and horrible nowadays.

The personnel vetting in our office was carried out by the executive. They're a pretty good lot, and they tried to process us as humanly as possible. Simply wrote on every file 'Socio-political attitude satisfactory'. Very decent. No-one felt compromised, disgraced, forced into anything. The whole thing went very smoothly. But there are filthy rotters everywhere. We appeared before the board. They read out their findings and each of us went off satisfied. Not Herczak, though. When his turn came, he nearly choked with indignation. ' "Socio-political attitude satisfactory!" Me, a wholehearted, committed party member, son of a worker who fought against oppression before the war, and father of two citizens carrying out responsible assignments on the political and economic front.'

The bloody twister, his elder son is in the personnel department at some works, the other one's a driver, drives the director of a big food concern. Herczak went on, listing his services to the state. Just think of it! The man's no good at his job, his projects always have to be altered, he's lazy, always off work with a doctor's note.

The board were taken aback. This was one they weren't prepared for. After much haggling, they rewrote the opinion so that it read like a eulogy for this model communist, emphasizing that, in the difficult conditions of martial law, he had shown exceptionally good judgement and exemplary initiative. In my view, the man's a camouflaged Ubek, who's dropped his mask at last. Our military commissioner, a young major, a decent enough guy, told the director in confidence that the security were getting out of hand and even the military didn't find it easy to put them back on the leash. Let alone muzzle the murderous pack altogether. But I dare say they all shift the blame on to somebody else.

The tea at least was fine. Maria had got in a stock of Madras and Assam before December. She's always hoarded things like a squirrel. It's paid off though. A car engine had been roaring away for some time. That thug on the ground floor was tinkering with his Polonez again. Revs it up with the throttle wide open. Doesn't give a damn about anybody. I felt like leaning out of the window and giving him a piece of my mind.

'Leave it alone,' said Maria.

The noise stopped anyhow. He's another fishy character. Nobody knows what he does. Never stops grinning. Seems to have grown even happier since this war started.

I switched the telly on for the news. Just pressed the knob out of habit, and away we went! Rubbish and lies. Seemed worse than ever somehow. The newsreaders' ugly mugs were solemn and unctuous. They mouthed their words lovingly, uttering slanders, insults, and threats with pedantic care. How hideous they are! What disgusting, wormeaten phizogs! After the news, a short story from life, they said. Some collaborators purporting to speak on behalf of the workers in a plant making presses. Everything very satisfactory, production going up, sense of relief all round, calm and order at last. I happen to know the place: we have had dealings with them for years. They were given a thorough 'pacification' on 13 December and two weeks afterwards workers were still being hauled out of their homes at night. They are still protesting, nonetheless. Stop work for five, ten minutes. Dead silence in the machine-room. The hounds are then let loose to find out who the ringleaders are. The workers don't let on. Everyone has a good story: no oil, had to let it cool down, had to adjust a screw . . . Must be two 'realities': one on the telly, the other in real life. It's unbearable. Here am I: I've just come away from 'life', I sit down in front of the telly, and a different world opens up before my eyes. Next, a fat hairless crook posing as a sage came on to give the rationale of the state of war. A professor, a philosopher, according to the announcer. I felt blood rushing to my head. Throbbing, pressure at the temples.

'You bastard!' I couldn't take any more. 'How dare you dish out that crap! I hope you get lockjaw!'

'You're wasting your breath,' said Maria. 'He's just a piece of garbage. Don't be so silly.'

She was absolutely right. This way I'm letting myself be influenced by their propaganda. I got up to turn off this box of crap. Loud protest, from Asa this time. There was supposed to be a film later. At twelve, she has already learnt to sit in front of the box. She must be half poisoned by their vomit. Never mind, let Maria worry about her beloved daughter. She will bring her up to be an empty-headed telly moron.

'Oh, do what you like, I'm off.'

I went for a walk. The park is very close. And the old town. I could get some air, cool off a bit. The evening was warm and pleasant. Spring had come. Nature, at least, is looking better. Somebody wrote on the wall yesterday, 'Winter is yours – spring will be ours.' It's been painted over. Not properly, of course. You can still see it. They can't do anything properly. Everything they touch they make a mess of. Lots of people out for a walk. The young, embracing, whispering sweet nothings. Asa? She'll start going out with boys soon. May have started, for all I know. Fewer patrols. There used to be a checkpoint at the cross-roads, for pedestrians and cars. It's gone. Another lot used to lurk under the arches. They've gone too. The iron corset has been loosened a bit this last day or two. Fewer of them on the road. Wagons, trucks, radio cars. A column used to go down our street regularly every night. It was the same in other parts of the town. A show of strength, I suppose. Psychological pressure: we're here, there, and everywhere, wide awake, ever ready. I remember, only a week ago, in this park, I was walking along lost in thought and they appeared from nowhere, three of them. Papers! Took ages over it, lots of note-taking. Looked me over carefully. And all this at 9 p.m., long before the curfew. At least that chapter seems to be over.

A technician at work told me his story . . . He was going home after the curfew on foot. Lives a long way away.

Didn't bump into a patrol once. So they've loosened up a bit. But it doesn't mean a thing. They're lurking there in the background. Lying in ambush.

May jump out of the bushes at any time, appear from any gateway. They're skulking in every odd corner. They lie in wait, oil their rifles, their walkie-talkies are going all the time. They're ready! For what? The grass is getting greener. Like a carpet. Boys and girls on the benches. Billing and cooing. What a time to be young in! Life is so short. All sorts of illness may be waiting for you, and this diabolical system on top of it all. The guy who has a brother-in-law in the security said they would tighten up for May. They're bringing in extra militia, they've requisitioned all the hotels for them. They're in a funk about their so-called Labour Day. Don't want it to get out of control. Don't want to hear anybody speaking the truth. I imagined myself stealing up behind a militiaman on patrol. I tap him lightly on the shoulder, and say, 'Hello.'

He turns round nervously. I look at his face: it's Herczak, the twister. I grab him by the balls as hard as I can. He falls to the ground, foaming at the mouth. I trample on his overblown body.

I managed to drag myself away from this sadistic fantasy and walked faster. Almost jogging along the paths through the park. It was dark now. I imagined a man behind every bush. I thought every loud footstep was a patrol. Even civilians looked suspicious to me. It's not persecution mania. The peaceful-looking geezer may, just may, be one of them: I don't trust them an inch!

I slowed down. I was only out for a walk, after all.

The Mongrel

———————*———————

Today, the picture of the Black Madonna was to be brought to the parish church. The market square was decked with blue and yellow bunting. It was warm. People waiting for a bus basked in the sun. In front of them the bright market square and the massive church, with its cream-coloured walls. Spring had set in. The old poplars were in bud, pale green shoots were to be seen on the ground. People blinked like cats, enjoying themselves.

A sudden thrill ran through the bus queue like an electric current. A teenage boy was the first to notice.

'Look at that,' he called out.

All turned their heads.

The town hall was under repair and a white and red ribbon with 'Solidarity' written across it could be seen on the metal scaffolding. No-one had noticed when it actually appeared. The word stood out proudly, as lovely to look at as forbidden fruit. It fitted into the happily-composed picture: the clear sky, the blue and yellow bunting along the road the holy image was to be taken. It lit the place somehow.

The queue gazed at it, pleased. Many smiled. Some clapped.

'Hurrah!' someone shouted.

People were coming out onto the balconies. A holiday mood spread. A woman placed some flowers at the foot of the scaffolding. Daffodils.

It was at this moment they came into the square. Three of

91

them, two in uniform, one civilian. The uniformed pair walked along slowly, indolently. But the civilian rushed ahead. On short, bent legs, he trotted forward. Kept his head down, as if on a scent. A mongrel dog, that's what he looked like.

He was first at the scaffolding. The uniformed pair stood behind him. His arm was too short. Couldn't reach it. Tried jumping, touched the ribbon with his clawing hand. But fell back without it. Tried again. Several times. Leapt higher every time, snapping at the ribbon like a rabid dog. He crouched down, gathered all his strength, and hurled himself into the air. Reached it this time. Got his hand on it and pulled. Once, twice. Wrenched it, with manic force. Tore it off. Started rolling it up, crumpled it in his hands, pushed it inside his coat. Wiped the sweat off his face, exhausted. Noticed the flowers on the ground. Stamped on them in a rage. The task completed, they left. The uniformed pair in front this time, the little civilian following.

Someone in the crowd put his finger in his mouth and let out a piercing whistle. Others joined in. The civilian shrank visibly. Walked faster. The people's laughter struck his back. He was in front now. The two in uniform followed, still at the same leisurely pace. He was almost running.

So much for the spring scene. The square ready to receive the holy picture. The Solidarity ribbon. And those three: two well-set-up, well-fed thugs in uniform, with a runt of a civilian in tow. A mongrel on a leash. Except that the leash was invisible.

The Forest

———————————————*———————————————

It wasn't by any means a primeval forest. Yet it had its mysteries. Clearings hidden among the ancient pines. Sandy hillocks amid the marshes. Ravines overrun by silver birch. These places had remained undisturbed for many years. Unbroken silence reigned there. To reach them you had to wind your way through thickets of briars, climb over old tree trunks brought down by storms, stumble on black ponds among the rushes. You passed flourishing colonies of dark mushrooms and red fungi.

The forest was surrounded by fields and human settlements. Though ruthless axes had hacked at its fringes it held on stubbornly and retained some of its beauty. It was a paradise for the village boys, who kept turning up battered helmets and bayonets from more than one war.

The forest had its free inhabitants too. You would suddenly glimpse the white scut of a vanishing roe or buck. Wild boar lived in wet hazel groves; their tusks left deep furrows in the ground. The village women in search of bilberries avoided those parts with care. At dusk, local people often saw a fox taking a short cut. Every year, the first snow made the map of bird and animal life clear for all to see: the tangle of footprints, the cross-stitching of claw marks led by labyrinthine paths to the heart of the forest.

With the years, signs of life in the forest grew rarer. The animal population had been mercilessly reduced by hunters. Shooting parties surrounded whole tracts of the forest, sent in dogs and blazed away. The forest itself shrank and thinned out. Wedges of cleared ground were driven deeper and deeper, and bare patches with a fuzz of underbrush covered much of the area.

The forest was dying. The old secret clearings, once rarely visited by sunlight filtering through the lofty crowns of ancient trees, were exposed and robbed of all their beauty.

By a sandy island in the marshland where only stunted pines grew, their roots miraculously clinging to the ground, a cinder track was laid and a derrick erected. They were drilling for oil. The throbbing of the drill scared the birds away. A pair of buzzards used to live in a hollow sculpted by lightening in a dead tree. They have gone with the others.

The silver birch glen survived longest. It somehow evaded man's destructive attentions. It was still possible, on an autumn day, to walk along its narrow path to the rustle of dry leaves. To hide in this retreat and to meditate in its perfect lonely silence. But last winter the whirring of chain saws hemmed in the glen. The wood-cutters had found their way to the trees which formed a semicircle around the birch copse. The crash and rumble of falling timber continued through the winter. Some trunks were taken off by tractor, others sawn up and stacked. The picturesque glen was no more. Just a ragged claypit littered with empty tins, wine bottles, and a few stranded, stunted birches. The bigger trees had been razed to the ground. The forest was a forest no more, but a great naked clearing, with a few saplings scattered about. Prefabricated houses, grey and ugly, loomed everywhere. Beyond them, a flat, empty plain spread out to the horizon.

A young man, who used to muse and dream in the clearings, stood now on a sandy hillock, perhaps a sacred mound of the ancients, among the marshes. He scanned the bald, devastated ground. His face hardened, eyes glittered coldly. There was nothing left to bind him to this land. Nothing but memories. Not once did he look back as he walked away.

Judas in the Square

———————— * ————————

They looked bored. You could see it. Three healthy bulls, swaying, flexing their knees. One stroked his club, the other scratched his behind, the third pawed the ground, horse-like.

'Looking for trouble,' Piotrowski stated. Without so much as a goodbye, he was off, quick as a deer.

'Looking for trouble,' repeated Jas Bobrzak. In a funk.

The city was still in turmoil. Water cannons were still at it here and there. Smoke billowed from the big stores. The siren of a patrol car pierced the air. What was that fire? Were people still burning red flags? In the square itself, it was all over. Deserted. Only a few people at the bus stop. The whole square cordoned off by the riot squads. Wagons and men at the ready.

'We should cross now,' said Jas. Started biting his nails again. Always did when nervous. He could still see Piotrowski among the people across the square.

But the hairdresser wouldn't play.

'You know where I work! They wouldn't touch me!'

He worked in the barber's shop at the Army Staff Building.

'We aren't mixed up in any of this. We're just walking towards the station.' The hairdresser sounded cool.

He still had faith in his chums, the army. He had some officer friends. Cut their hair and shaved them, let them jump the queue. They reciprocated. Only a few days ago a major he knew had told him where he could get windscreen wipers for his Fiat at a bargain price.

'Okay,' sighed Jas.

They set off. Walking straight towards the three thugs. They were perhaps fifty metres away. The street was empty. The crowd, swept off the square, was milling around on the other side. On their side, only the wagons and those three.

Jas felt more and more uneasy. As though he was in no man's land. Such a narrow strip between themselves and wagons full of riot troops.

'We're walking into a minefield,' he mumbled.

The hairdresser was unmoved. Went on with his story about a bird called Grazyna. He had run into her in a bar.

'Turns me on, this bird,' he kept on repeating.

A regular guy, the hairdresser. Pink, piggy face, fair hair, bright blue eyes, bulging a bit. His eyes always look surprised.

They were close now. The thugs weren't looking. They stood sideways, watching the fire at the other end of the square. One was shading his eyes with his hand.

The sun shone straight into their faces.

Jas saw them in sharp outline. Only too well. Relaxed but alert. Muscles tensed. One wrong step and they would pounce. The plastic visors were up, and they held their plastic shields. Their machine pistols were slung across their chests. And then they had clubs. Equipped like fortresses. But they managed to look light on their feet. Like fighting bulls.

Jas and the hairdresser were almost past them. Another metre or two. Jas was longing to speed up. Had to put brakes on his feet to stop them from running away with him. You have to walk nice and slowly. To avoid attracting attention. They were past! Jas half closed his eyes. Thank God! The hairdresser was right. They had made it.

That very second, he heard a 'hello!' Very leisurely, very slow. He cringed, and his heart gave a funny jerk, like a fish being landed.

'Did you hear?' he whispered to the hairdresser.

'Who says it's us they want?' smiled the hairdresser, all condescending.

'Hallo!' They heard it again.

The hairdresser turned first. Then Jas looked round cautiously.

The three thugs watched them. One stretched out a hand and beckoned.

'Come over here!' he said. It was the one who had been scratching his behind earlier on. Jas remembered him.

They came closer.

'What is it you want?' asked the hairdresser. He had stopped smiling at last.

They were both shorter than the militia. Had to look up. The tallest of the three spoke.

'Come nearer, will you?'

'What is this?' The hairdresser sounded surprised.

No reply. Still looking down on them. Still blinking. Although the sun was no longer in their eyes. It lasted for a second. Perhaps a few seconds. The tallest one took hold of the hairdresser's elbow. Fast. Professional. The hairdresser moaned.

'I work for the military!' he squeaked in a thin high voice.

'Says he works . . .' said the tall one wonderingly, '. . . for the military,' chuckled the other.

'Quite a bloke, eh?' And he patted the hairdresser on the shoulder.

'Take your hands off me!' The hairdresser pushed him away.

Another professional grip. The hairdresser squirmed and moaned again.

'What's this? Resisting? Causing an affray?'

The voice sounded like a caress. He caught the hairdresser by the collar. His eyes were clear and good humoured. He was very young.

98

'Must have something on his conscience, eh?'

The other two nodded.

The tall thug grabbed the hairdresser by the scruff of the neck. Squeezed his arm. The hairdresser's face was screwed up with pain, eyes bulging. He mumbled something.

'Abusive language, now! Insulting an officer on duty.' The tallest one stopped smiling. He screwed up his eye and barked, like a rabid dog:

'Get him out of here,' and pushed the hairdresser away.

The other two caught him under the arms.

With a kick or two they dragged him to the wagon. The hairdresser managed to turn his face, just for a second.

'Jas,' he shouted, '– Jas.'

They pushed him into the wagon. Then the tallest one looked at Jas. For the first time.

'You saw it? Resisting authority, causing a disturbance. Am I right?' His clear, watchful eyes hypnotized Bobrzak.

Jas's head felt empty. Sweat trickled down his back. He licked his lips. Nodded.

The tall thug expected more than a nod.

'Yes, I saw it,' whispered Jas. 'That's how it was.'

The tall thug smiled.

'You may go,' he waved his arm, lightly.

The arm holding the club.

Jas walked off, as ordered. He had betrayed the hairdresser. That's what he had done. He stooped, shrank. He was still aware of the tall one's presence behind him. He quickened his step.

The Steel-Clawed Glove

————————————— * —————————————

They had had a good journey. Only four of them in the compartment. The country looked fresh, alive with the first green of the spring. Not just peaceful: serene. It passed gently, rhythmically, across the carriage windows.

A stocky priest looked into the breviary opened on his knees, then raised his eyes and thrust his face closer to the window. Ploughing and sowing had started. The slow unalterable rhythm of peasant life. A man following a plough bent to the effort. Crows flew down onto the upturned soil.

A white horse was grazing in a meadow with a wood in the background. Pretty as a picture.

'A good horse,' said the old man in the navy blue uniform, gazing through the window.

There were two other passengers in the compartment. Neither of them took any interest in the view. The man wearing glasses seemed absorbed in the thick volume he was reading. His eyesight must have been very poor: he held the book close despite his glasses. A soldier, corporal's tabs on his shoulder, sat near the door. He had undone his belt, put his cap on the seat beside him. He sat with his head bent down. But he wasn't asleep. His short fingers drummed nervously on the arm of the seat. The middle finger carried a thick gold wedding ring.

The old man in uniform yawned. He looked round the compartment. His eyes rested on the priest for a moment. The priest's lips were moving. In prayer, no doubt.

'Yes,' said the old man, 'prayer is our only hope. Holy

scripture alone carries the truth. But not everything has been revealed yet . . .' He frowned and turned to watch the moving country outside. Cottages. A stork. Green trees. A tractor in a field track. Children waving handkerchiefs at the train.

The familiar scenes floated by. Life renewing itself, the same from year to year.

'How long will it go on?' The old man had difficulty in putting his words together. 'What can we do about it all? Only don't tell me, Father, that we need compassion and patience and humility!' His faded blue eyes clouded over.

The priest sighed and spread his hands helplessly.

The man in glasses, until then absorbed in a thick volume with an exotic god on the dust jacket spouting liquid fire from his funnelled mouth, broke off his reading. With the gesture of a practised reader, he pushed a finger between the pages and closed the book.

'I'm reading about the Aztec state, about Montezuma, about priests tearing children's hearts out to sacrifice them to their gods. The Spaniards were only a handful, yet they crushed the mighty empire of the sun! And without much difficulty.' He banged his hand on the closed book. His face was thin, birdlike, and behind the thick glasses the eyes blinked incessantly with a nervous tic. 'That empire was built on slavery, injustice. It was rotten. Cortez had the will to win and nothing to lose!'

'Like the proletariat,' said the old man. 'The empire had nothing to lose but its chains.'

The corporal raised his head. But not to look at his fellow passengers. He concentrated on the opposite wall, which was embellished with an advertisement for Orbis restaurant cars. He looked tense. His lips were tight, his legs were drawn up uncomfortably.

The old man gave the soldier a careful, appraising glance.

'Don't worry so much, soldier,' he said gently. He took

his briefcase down from the shelf. Opened it. Took out a bottle filled with an opaque yellow liquid. Pushed it towards the soldier. 'Cheer up, corporal. I made it myself. With sugar.'

The corporal accepted the bottle and took a hefty swig of moonshine. Didn't even pull a face. Wiped his mouth with the back of his hand.

'The buggers! They've postponed our discharge for a year.' His apathetic eyes lit up with rage. 'It's a year since I saw my kid. Got a pass now the kid's ill. I don't know what things are like at home, how my kid's going on.' The tension made him clench his teeth, the veins stood out on his hands.

'My own boy,' said the old man in his quiet voice, 'worked down the mine. They've put him in clink. Three years he got.'

The corporal shied, and looked at the old man with anxious, hunted eyes. He pulled at the old man's sleeve with his red, frostbitten hand.

'I had nothing to do with all that. Not me. The riot squads, the militia took the mines. We were only in reserve, I swear it.' In desperation, he turned to the others. They kept silent and looked away.

'It's all right, lad.' The old man placed his large heavy hand over the corporal's. 'I bear no grudges. Are *they* to blame?' The question was directed at the priest.

The priest closed his breviary.

'Even the militia,' the old man said thoughtfully '– they're only a blind tool . . .'

The man in glasses cleared his throat and said in a near whisper:

'Here we are. Spring's coming. The journey is comfortable. No crowds. We trust one another. And what good is it all?' He looked out of the window. 'It's terrible! It's all so terrible!'

The old man pushed the bottle towards the soldier again. But he wouldn't have any more.

'No, thank you. Makes you feel better for a bit but then it's worse than ever.'

The old man pushed the cork back and returned the bottle to his battered briefcase. He fastened the straps. Carefully replaced it on the shelf.

'You're quite right,' the priest spoke for the first time. 'They are only a blind tool.'

'When they went in to storm the mine,' said the old man, 'they looked like devils. The gloves they had on,' his hand stretched out, the fingers wide apart, '– they had claws, of steel. If they got you in those claws, you'd had it. You'd never break loose from them.'

The man in glasses stared at the cruel, clutching fingers. 'Claws of steel,' he repeated in a whisper.

They sat in silence. The country outside darkened. The paw with steel claws hovered over them. They could feel them, claws that raked body and soul.

The old man shut his eyes. The corporal curled up in his corner.

The train sped over the green plain. Spring had come.

A Short Street

———————————※———————————

The beauty shop occupied premises in the corner building at the bottom of the street. Outside, a fat woman pushed half a cigarette into a glass holder and inhaled fiercely. The queue in front of the shop was short, fifteen people or so. There was a good chance, she thought. She joined the queue. In front of her, two teenagers were absorbed in conversation.

The fat woman moved her weight from one foot to the other. She had varicose veins and the pain in her calves was incessant. She could catch odd fragments of the boys' conversation. One of them had just come out of hospital and was telling his story. The fat woman had seen something of hospitals in her time and she listened with interest.

The boy lowered his head to demonstrate the fresh, pink scar of a semicircular incision in the scalp.

'I had a blood clot on the brain,' he said. 'Concussion.'

The fat woman pushed the other half of her cigarette into the holder and lit up. She tried to get a look at the boy's face. No luck. The boy was standing with his back to her.

'It was great really. I had a splendid time: doctors, nurses, everyone dancing attendance.'

A car stopped opposite the shop. A tall, fair girl, in high boots and very tight trousers got out. She was walking nonchalantly, playing with the car keys.

The boy broke off his story. They all looked round at the girl. The fat woman smiled blissfully. Her varicose veins had stopped hurting just for the moment.

A shop assistant in a blue apron appeared in the doorway. 'No more soap,' he announced loudly.

The queue started to disperse. Some cursed their luck. The face of the fat woman grew red, and she gasped soundlessly like a fish out of water. With her shaky hands she took from her bag a small piece of grey soap wrapped in newspaper.

'It stinks! They allowed us a hundred grammes each at work! The cleaner won't even scrub the lavatory with it.' She threw the soap down on the pavement and stamped on it in a rage. 'Stinks like rotten fish!' she kept saying, her voice hoarse from her exertions.

The shop assistant in the blue apron stood on the steps, and laughed noisily.

The street was a short one. At the other end, another odd scene was taking place.

A grey, bent man in glasses stopped and turned round to have a look at a passing militiaman: a tall chap, laden with an automatic, a truncheon, a dagger, and a rucksack. He was lame and duck-footed.

'Looks as if somebody's shoved a stick up his arse,' said the man in glasses. 'They don't wash their feet for weeks on end, no wonder they get raw.' The old man cackled maliciously, and looked around hoping that someone had heard him.

Two plumbers were at work nearby repairing a well. They hadn't heard. There was some sort of stoppage. They swore hideously.

The pigeons were at the centre of a third happening. They have become very lazy. They flock together in the roadway in large numbers and won't budge. Warming themselves in the spring sun. They take off in a leisurely way from under the wheels of oncoming vehicles.

A taxi driver, an elderly man, stopped his cab, leant out of the window and elaborately cursed the lumbering birds.

His oaths were of the sort usually reserved for humans. He moved off only when the queue of cars behind started sounding their horns.

'Sons of bitches!' he said. His eyes were ablaze with fury and blind to the astonished faces of his passengers.

'People are very jumpy nowadays,' one elderly lady informed another. Her eyes were still quick and she made a careful detour to avoid the grey soapy smear on the pavement. She wondered for a moment whether it was a dog's mess. No, it looked like something else. The two elderly ladies continued blithely down the street, studying the shop windows as they went.

Squad Ready for Action

————————————— * —————————————

A hurricane will sometimes fell the biggest oaks and leave a sapling standing.

He was a man of strong character and a rich past. They had failed to break him in all those years. Failed to tear out the core of his soul. The Stalinist period was his darkest hour. He had lived in hiding, wasn't included in any amnesty. His two bravura escapes were well known and much admired. One from the NKVD. The other from our own Bezpieka. His wife, who was overweight and unwell, became miraculously young again – a gazelle as he used to call her – whenever she remembered even earlier days, the time of the German Occupation. That was when she met the tall, good-looking young man in riding boots and breeches, a second lieutenant of the Underground Army of whom her younger brother always spoke with unqualified admiration. Not surprisingly, they got married, with the usual wartime haste. They lived on danger and courage. She worked as a courier for the provincial command, he lived up to his pseudonym, 'The Bold'. They could talk for hours about the adventures of those days, interrupting one another.

The years after the war were just as hectic, and they hardly noticed the transition. As far as they were concerned the war was still on. Life was still a sequence of actions, provocateurs, narks, heroes, cowards, friends and foes. They chucked details at one another, places, names, pseudonyms. The stamping of nailed boots, shootings, individual or by categories, camps in the forest, little attic rooms where they spent days of excruciating boredom longing for nightfall. The new rulers were invariably referred to as 'the communist rabble, lackeys'. The words were pronounced with a contemptuous, aristocratic intonation. That's what they were like. Tough. Unswervingly loyal. Their personal life had consisted of short, stolen meetings, brief embraces, and partings for many years after the war had ended. There was one long-lasting hurt. The death of their first child, a six-month-old boy. True, the birth of another child very soon afterwards brought solace. The second boy's arrival had given her new strength. It was his dream to pass on to his only child the principles, the values he had been taught in the underground officers' training school. He believed in continuity.

He used a sporting metaphor: he liked to call it handing on the baton to the next generation. That's where the nation's strength lay. Each defeated generation replaced by the next magnificent contingent, rising like the phoenix from its ashes. He saw his son in that historic procession. He would be the boy's caring adviser, would share with him the experience gained from all the years he had given to the fatherland.

He had in mind an ideal picture of his successor. His ardent and imperious longing decreed that his heir could have no other destiny. The boy had a strong character. Everybody said so. His father's son. He also resembled him physically. Unfortunately, the longed-for continuity went no further. The son used his strength for bad purposes. His regular companions were wide boys and social misfits. In his circle the only purpose of existence was to get hold of money for girls and drink. Naturally, there was no moral code to observe. Betrayals, and secret collaboration with the police, were common occurrences. The struggle between father and son was a stubborn one. Two strong, explosive personalities. Never sparing one another. The son moved out of the family flat. The father thought that he would be back soon with his tail between his legs. Nothing of the sort. The boy had no intention of going back. His mother helped him on the quiet. The father guessed as much, but pretended he knew nothing. It was easier that way, less hurtful to his pride. Besides, a small flame of paternal feeling still flickered. The boy certainly had strength of character. And that was a quality his father prized. The quality which determined his judgement of people in general. The boy would change, would mature. He would start thinking and see that his father was right. No other outcome was possible. The mother tried to mediate. She presented each party's terms to the other. She softened the 'no' which was the father's invariable reaction. The boy returned home. After much resistance, he accepted his father's main condition: he had to find work. He became an agent for a firm specializing in winter-proofing windows. For the father, this was yet another slap in the face. What a job! Call that work? But he bore his humiliation in furious silence.

'I am working, am I not?' the boy asked sweetly.

Yes, he was working. His father had to admit it. There was a grain of consolation. The boy was fighting. He hadn't surrendered. There were even moments when his father could imagine him in a wartime setting. Loose overcoat – preferably a raglan – riding boots, a cap. One of those troublesome heroes of the underground who had to be held down, whose daring had to be curbed. He began to see himself in his child again.

The state of war, declared on 13 December, pushed the family drama into the background. When the father heard the news he didn't believe it at first. Never quite believed it. This strange war hemmed him in. Telephones cut off. The clatter of soldiers' boots. Tanks and gun barrels. Internment, arrests. All played out in a frosty, wintry setting. He looked through the window. Maybe he saw the camp at Z. in 1945. Wire, observation turrets, guards. It was a prison camp for soldiers of the Home Army picked up by the Russians. He had managed to escape in the spring. Those he left behind were sent to Siberia.

He now spent hours lying on the sofa, never switching the light on, not even listening to the news. Mother and son in the other room spent hours at the radio, trying to pick the Voice of America or the BBC out of the jamming and the polyglot babble. He didn't want to listen. Best of all he liked lying with his face to the wall. Yet until this strange war started he had never wavered in his geopolitical optimism. 'The Reds are bound to fall. They will disintegrate. The end of their empire is at hand,' he used to say. Now he had simply ceased to react. Good and bad news was the same to him. His face looked grey and sunken, his eyes had no lustre. A ruin. That's what he looked like. A natural ruin perhaps. A tree buffeted by the whirlwind. Torn up by the roots. He was failing. A film of apathy over the face, slumped shoulders, the movements of an old man. Until recently, he had held himself well, and had seemed to be in excellent physical condition, age notwithstanding. 'You look like a trapper, or a Canadian lumberjack,' his son had said a short while ago. It had given him much pleasure.

He no longer took any interest in the boy. The young man's life style hadn't changed. He was constantly visited by his dubious friends, fixers and wasters. In the old days the father used to chase them away – open the door and bark 'Be off with you!' They left meekly like cowed dogs. Now they sat in his son's room, drinking and behaving noisily as if they were in a bar. He could hear them. They were discussing their shady deals. He could hear girls squealing. Even the mother, who had taken her son's side in the past, was loud in her disapproval.

'Like a den of thieves,' she said in disgust.

'Where do you want us to meet? They've closed all the joints,' was the boy's answer.

'You ought to do something about it,' she said to her husband.

He was lying on the sofa, as usual. Didn't even turn his head. She was getting anxious about his condition. This had gone on too long. She talked to a woman friend, a doctor. The friend quoted a Latin medical name for his condition, and suggested a visit to a psychiatrist. They sat in the kitchen and whispered conspiratorially.

Christmas Eve saw something of a miracle. He had always loved the Christmas tradition. In the past, even when ill or worried, he had cheered up at Christmas, as if at the touch of a magic wand.

The day was full of surprises. He got up quite early, washed and shaved. Had a look at the record-player. Pushed a pile of pop records aside in disgust.

'Have you got any carols?' he asked.

After a long search his son found a record with all the old favourites.

He then discussed with his wife in great detail the programme for the evening. First, the menu. Any difficulties were met with a firm, 'We'll have to pay a bit more, we have to get hold of the right stuff.' He himself took charge of the drink. Went out for the first time in days. Spent a long time in the foreign-currency shop. Came back with a case of the best vodka. His son gave him a look of surprised respect. His wife a look of relief. He seemed a different man.

When they sat down to Christmas Eve dinner he was the first to raise his glass to his son. They drank together. Was this a symbol? Peace? They started drinking seriously. They didn't talk much. The son was suspicious, at first. Watched his father from the corner of his eye. The alcohol took care of that. They warmed to one another. The father

avoided referring to the boy's habits. He didn't make sar-
castic remarks about his job. Had he come to terms with
'the pits', as he usually called his son's world? He did say
one rather strange thing:

'It makes no difference what anybody does.' Waved his
hand towards the dark outside. 'It's a wilderness full of
wolves. It isn't worth knocking yourself out.'

This pessimistic remark had no sequel. Christmas spirit
prevailed.

The vodka worked fast. His eyes sparkled, full of life. He
paced the room, with stiff, unnatural steps. Suddenly he
leant over the boy.

'What are they like?' he asked, and squeezed his shoulder.

'Who?'

'Those chums of yours, Neon, Yogi, Mix . . .' He
remembered all their nicknames.

The boy looked happy. He loved talking about his friends.

'Yogi is as strong as a bear.' He was so pleased! The first
time his father had taken a serious interest in his life. 'He
can lift a guy up and throw him about like a ball. A hundred
kilograms is nothing to him. He's done some wrestling.
He's devoted to me. Like a faithful dog. You tell him to
wait somewhere, he will wait for hours. Till he's called off.
That's what he's like. Slow, thick, but he doesn't know
what fear means. Now Mix! There's a guy for you! Once,
we were in a bar together. Kasia was with us. A thug
pinched Kasia's bum. "Beautiful bum," he said, "a masterpiece." "She's my girl," says Mix, pretending to be almost
crying. He looks like a square. Wears glasses. "Shut up,
you little shrimp, or I'll wring your neck." "Oh dear,"
moaned Mix feebly. The thug tried to hit him. That's all
Mix was waiting for. He ducked and let fly with a left and a
right. The other chap went down like a ninepin. "Kicked
me," was all he could say. Mix's punch is like a kick from a
horse, right enough.'

The father listened attentively.

'That's great,' he said with satisfaction.

'The others are okay too. Jurek, for instance. Likes playing jokes on the militia.'

The father pushed the tots away and poured the stuff into tumblers. The son broke off.

'Have a drink. This is how we used to drink in the forest. Rotgut, of course. So you've got these three pals, the three musketeers?'

'I've got at least ten. I haven't told you about them all.'

'A patrol. Ten. Well, the thing is to drill them, give them a bit of discipline, train them in urban warfare, different forms of it. Do you realize how much you can do with ten or a dozen? You could disarm . . . a checkpoint.'

'Sir!' The son sprang to attention. 'Squad ready for action!'

'Qui~t, you young pup,' scolded the father. 'I want to see them tomorrow. All together, understood?'

The young man nodded eagerly. Poured out more drink. Later, very drunk, they simply exchanged inarticulate sounds. And gestures. They understood one another perfectly.

The father fell asleep first. Over the table. His head dropped into the plate with the remains of the Carp Nelson. He snored. The young man took him under the arms and dragged him to the sofa. Still able to sit up, he lit a cigarette.

'Squad ready for action!' he managed to stammer.

His head lolled. The cigarette was still burning in the corner of his mouth. He was smiling. The record-player was still on, and the words of the carol were 'Christ is born'.

The Soldiers and the Girl

————————————— * —————————————

The city came to life in the evening. During the day the heat drove everyone down to the river or else into hiding somewhere in the shade. The sun set in a red glow. It meant another scorcher. Only at dusk did the air get cooler, stirred by light breezes. Everybody went out for a stroll. Animals too, half asleep and only half alive in the heat of the day, showed more spirit as darkness fell. Dogs gambolled, cats emerged from cellars and hiding places among the rubbish dumps. But even in the evening a quickened step or any sudden movement drenched the body with sweat. People moved as little as possible, drifting lazily around, lightly dressed in vests, shorts, and sandals. They sat around in back gardens or the local parks. Three weeks of heatwave! The harvest was at risk because of the drought. There were reports of forest fires. Old people complained of high blood pressure and heart troubles. But the young loved it. They luxuriated in the sun and water. Everyone was slack and idle. Thoughts slowed down, troubles and worries seemed less pressing. The heatwave had its good points. Ambling along in the dark you could hear water trickling from flower boxes on the balconies. Through the windows you saw naked figures moving about inside. Here and there an electric fan hummed. Life had acquired a tropical rhythm.

The sight of open trucks filled with soldiers was a regular evening event. No-one knew where they were going. But the trucks appeared late every evening, with absolute regularity. Perhaps just to warn us all that they were there, on the alert.

That night a heavy truck rumbled down the road at the usual time. They were driving through. Ranged on seats along both sides of the truck. Six on one side and six on the other, swaying rhythmically. Faces shining with sweat. Helmets, Kalashnikovs hanging across their chests, heavy uniforms. The officer in charge sat alone, between the two rows, with his back against the driver's cab. He wore a helmet like the others, but instead of a Kalashnikov had a revolver in a holster. Their vacant eyes roamed over the passing buildings and they were silent, tired, and apathetic. The officer sagged in a crumpled heap.

The truck stopped at the lights. A few pedestrians had been waiting to cross. An old man with a mongrel dog. A young man carrying a child piggyback. Someone else.

Then a girl stepped onto the crossing. She walked like a dancer. The street light at the corner shone on her. She was bronzed by the sun and her tan contrasted vividly with her white shorts and shirt. Her breasts were taut against the blouse and shifted provocatively under the thin material. Her hips were wide and strong, her legs long. She walked with a light, firm step. Seemed almost to float through the heavy, thick air of the summer night. Probably just been seeing her boyfriend? She shook back her long, fair hair, tossing her head in a colt-like movement. She registered the presence of the soldiers without interest.

That dead army truck had suddenly come to life. The driver leaned out of the window. The two rows of soldiers moved as one man. Those on the left turned their heads as though at a word of command, those on the right raised themselves from their bench. They drank in the beauty of that summer apparition.

The girl didn't even look in their direction. Yet she couldn't have failed to feel those admiring eyes on her body. A woman has a sixth sense for the greedy yearning of the male.

The soldiers, imprisoned in the cage of their daily discipline, constrained by heavy winter uniforms, in their metal helmets and stiff leather belts, weighed down by the weaponry they had to carry, watched her like dogs chained day and night. They stared greedily, and her body must have become for them a tingling memory. A comfort on long, evil-smelling nights in barracks. The memory of that unattainable vision might surface one day over vodka. There would be blows and curses.

The lights changed. The truck was in no hurry to cross. After a while it went on down the paved street. The two rows of helmeted heads bobbed in unison again.

The sky was a beautiful dark blue, almost navy blue, filled with glowing constellations, the Great Bear, Cassiopeia and others, like luminous diamonds suspended over the planet.

The June Cross

————————————— * —————————————

Money was no trouble. So long as it was done on the quiet. Some slipped it into my pocket so deftly I didn't even know who they were. Especially the blokes who come in from the villages. Others made a lot of fuss. Wasiak, for one.

'Wife, kids, grandchildren. If I get found out, I'm finished . . .' But he still paid. A lot, for him: three hundred. Some party members also coughed up: on the quiet, without witnesses.

How many would turn up on the day? There was no knowing. There were a few I could rely on. The young chaps from the tool-room. Do a lot of moonlighting. Keen as mustard. Unless they'd had too much to drink the night before and overslept. Which was quite likely.

I woke the boy up. I had some trouble in rousing him. He's never been up so early, of course. Four o'clock. Just beginning to get light. The world looks pretty dismal at that hour. We had coffee. I lit up. The smoke felt sharp on an empty stomach. What if they didn't turn up? The two of us wouldn't be able to manage. Carry a cross that size, stand it up and fix it by ourselves? Much too heavy. Big pine trunks. The forester chose them himself and told us to chop them down. Like everyone else, 'If there's trouble, I know nothing.' The curate might lend a hand and the village beggar. If the parish priest lets them.

We walked through the empty, sleeping town. Not even a dog barked.

When we were putting the cross together in the churchyard we'd had no end of helpers. Wouldn't be right to deny it. But it's safe there, next door to the church. The young curate had helped. A fantastic bloke, can put his hand to anything. The parish priest wasn't all that pleased.

'No good tempting the devil! Better wait a while.'

Wait? For what? The clergy are also in two minds: some are OK, some conform.

I told at least forty men. Some only shook their heads. One said he couldn't: promised his mates to go fishing. Another had a christening to go to. The peasant workers live too far away. Busy on their own plots on Sundays and their wives wouldn't let them out.

They got my goat with their shilly-shallying.

'Don't you know, you bastards, what happened in June? Workers' blood was spilt!' After that they ran away at the sight of me.

Most people heard me out and said nothing. Would they turn up or wouldn't they? Damned if I knew. We walked through the empty streets of our little town. A night patrol might have stopped us. If they did, we were on our way to early mass. The boy was almost running. I had some difficulty keeping up. He loved it. An adventure. Dying to be mixed up in anything a bit risky. He's the right age. We old ones lack fire. We grow wary, get the shits for no reason at all. Yet, when we were making the cross, there were plenty of willing helpers. Everybody's brave, next door to the church. With sanctuary at hand. They haven't started barging into churches yet. A beautiful cross it was. We had stripped the trunks and painted them black, with a ribbon round the middle, 'To the memory of those who fell in June 1956.' The worst part was still to come: carrying it out and putting it up. I could be sure only of the four of us. Myself, the boy, the curate, and the beggar. But four wasn't enough.

People were scared. Some might have been called in and warned. A civilian in Security put me through it last week.

'What are you up to?' he kept on asking.

'Nothing,' I said. 'A religious matter.'

'Mind you don't slip up,' said he. 'Plenty of room inside for troublemakers like you.'

They might let me down, blast them. It's one thing to give money. Anonymously. Quite another to be seen putting up a cross in the square. The boy offered to bring in his mates, the scouts. I wouldn't hear of it. I wouldn't have them take the risk. They have interned children under age before now. Let the kids wait in the wings. For the time being, anyhow.

We approached the church from the presbytery. That's where we were going to meet. Under the old lime tree. My heart was pounding. Would they be there? I couldn't see at first. But they were! Sheltering behind a wall. Wegrzyniak. Lame Jack. Kajetaniak. Szymanski. The foreman from the tool-room. Two sorters. The moonlighters. I felt better. Well done. I shook everyone by the hand.

'More will be coming,' said Lame Jack.

Kajetaniak was drunk. Brought his axe with him. Staggered about and kept on repeating, 'Let me get at the thugs, and I'll smash their heads in . . .' He brandished the axe.

What a warrior! He's one of the peasant-workers. Drunk or not, he'd managed to get there.

'Quiet, quiet,' I said. 'I can't see any of that lot here.'

How had he managed to get drunk so early? At home, I suppose. The peasants make their own liquor. There were quite a few boozy breaths, beside Kajetaniak's, anyhow. They must've had one or two.

The foreman spat into his hand and set down to organize the work. The man has got his head screwed on all right. Knew what was what.

Then the technician, the one who had arranged to go fishing, appeared, short of breath.

'Fish can wait. Here I am.'

Kajetaniak was at it again. Brandishing the axe.

'Let them come, the sons of bitches and I'll deal with the lot of them!'

The young curate must have heard some of it, I'm afraid, because he joined us just at that moment.

I called the drunk to order.

'No need to swear. And you'd better have a bit of shut-eye out of the way somewhere.'

'I'm here to work, not sleep,' he answered.

They were lifting the cross by now. One, two. One, two . . . The foreman from the tool-room gave them their time. We carried it into the square. No problems. Kajetaniak thought better of it though: sat under a wall and snored away. Safer that way, for sure.

The sun was rising. It was going to be a nice day.

Hatred

————————— * —————————

Yesterday was a day of great drama and anger. It was the twenty-fifth anniversary of the workers' protest in Poznan. The crowds were immense, the square in front of the cathedral packed. The militia charged to disperse the demonstrators. I don't need to go into details. Everybody knows what happens on these occasions: smoke bombs, jets of water under high pressure, truncheons, groans, yells, crowds scattering blindly, the sirens of patrol cars. The scene is only too familiar. Except that yesterday the crowd seemed more recklessly excitable than on other occasions. More determined. They had obviously forgotten what fear was. Again and again, they charged the militia cordon until its iron ranks caved in under the pressure of that human avalanche. Bare-handed civilians traded blows with the heavily-armed knights of the Zomo.[1] The demonstrators had allies. Residents of the houses overlooking the square hung out of windows and hurled at the militia whatever came to hand. Things were improving, I thought. Till then, people had watched the militia's encounters with demonstrators in sullen silence. This time, they joined in. Jars of preserves seemed a favourite weapon. Laboriously-garnered jams, fruits, pickles were recklessly squandered. Jars descended on the militiamen's heads, shoulders, backs, made gaps in the serried ranks and diverted their attention. Vertical as well as horizontal vigilance was necessary. It reduced their effectiveness. While they were looking

[1] Acronym for the riot squads of the militia.

upwards, spying out the enemy at the windows, attackers from below caught them off guard and forced them back.

I rushed with the crowd through streets, alleyways, squares and courtyards, swept along by the heaving human multitude. I tried to stay in the rear, rather than pushing into the front line. Even so I saw a lot. I was able to observe the spontaneous emergence of leaders, tribunes of the people who lifted our spirits by their own courage. In the square in front of the cathedral a young standard-bearer waved a red and white sheet. He was exhorting the crowd to advance. A slight young man with an eloquent, determined face. Schoolboy, student? Then I saw a remarkably dextrous man in oily overalls, straight from the bench, give an acrobatic display throwing back the tear gas bombs shot at the crowd by the Zomo. He picked them up with bare hands as they rolled, hot and smoking, along the pavement, and hurled them at the attackers. He did this time after time. The Zomo cried and coughed. A cloud of smoke separated them from the crowd. They could see nothing. I also saw some suspicious characters. A repulsive-looking middle-aged man called for a blood bath and shouted outrageous anti-Soviet slogans. I was quite close to him. He stank of vodka: artificial courage, provided by his masters, I thought. There was no applause. People eyed him with distrust. Only a handful of dubious figures rallied round him. They disappeared almost as soon as they arrived. *Agents provocateurs?* I also saw old people behaving with unexpected bravery, transformed as if by magic into demons of action. Old women, disabled men. 'Thrash the bastards,' screamed the women, clawing with their rheumaticky fingers. Cripples lunged at the Zomo with sticks and artificial limbs.

I saw all that and much more in a kaleidoscopic sequence. But nothing stirred my imagination so much as an incident I observed in a narrow alley near the cathedral. Some of the demonstrators fleeing from the square had found their way there. The Zomo were on their heels. The alley led into a little square, from which it was the only escape route. People living in buildings on both sides came to the rescue. A shower of jars, pots, and other objects fell on the militia. I watched, spellbound. Then a man in his under-vest, roused perhaps from his afternoon nap, appeared on the third-floor balcony of the corner building. He was struggling with a large box of some sort. A television set! He lifted it with difficulty and rested it on the balustrade. He was red in the face: it must have been quite an effort. The box wobbled dangerously. He managed to steady it. At that moment the crowd gave way and the Zomo charged. A whole phalanx of them: water cannons, two trucks, and men armed with truncheons and flare pistols. The face of the man on the balcony twisted in a peculiar grimace. A grin of malicious glee. He braced himself against the balustrade, his eyes bulging, holding the set in both hands. He let go of the box, aiming at the men below. At the Zomo. My eyes closed involuntarily. It was a terrible moment. Blood, crushed bodies, broken skulls . . . There was a heavy thud and a grating noise. He had missed the men. The set had crashed on to one of the trucks, denting the roof as though it were a tin can. The vehicle stopped. The Zomo halted in confusion, ran over to see what had happened to those inside, then pulled themselves together and charged again. Just in time, I darted into a courtyard and climbed over a low wall. For the time being I was in a quiet street. But a moment later scuffles broke out there too. First came the tear gas bombs. Then, a hundred yards away, I saw another Zomo unit. Carried along by the surge of the crowd and the militia, by sudden assaults and equally sudden retreats, I found myself in a quiet quarter of small prewar houses and gardens. Still there was no peace. The smell of gas took my breath. My eyes watered. Flagstones had been torn up; there was glass everywhere. Then I saw a crowd of a few hundred young boys, some carrying national flags. They had mastered the knack of returning the bombs. Caught them almost in the air and threw them straight back at the militia. So it was mostly the Zomo who wept and writhed in the smoke. But the water cannons did their job. Jets like steel whips knocked people off their feet. I saw boys lying on the pavement. Vanquished by water! Unconscious, covered with blood. Unless friends managed to carry them into shelter, the Zomo moved in to batter their inert bodies with boot and truncheon. Drunk with the joy of battle. Lusting for revenge.

A single thick-set Zomo, pursuing the boys, rushed into the gardens behind the houses. Protected by a shield, wielding a truncheon in one hand and flare pistol in the other, he bounded into the gardens and glared about him, panting like a wild beast. The boys had disappeared. He looked around, wild-eyed. He banged his shield with his club in a bellicose frenzy. People watched him from the windows. When he realized he was being watched his face was contorted with rage. He foamed at the mouth. Quite literally. Foam trickled down from his lips. 'You sons of bitches,' he roared, and aimed the flare pistol at one of the windows. He missed. Luckily, a rustle among the lilacs had distracted him. He leapt into the bushes like a beast of prey. I heard him trampling, roaring inarticulately. But he emerged empty-handed. Nobody there. A solid lump of frustrated hatred, he ranged through the flower beds, borders, and vegetable patches, trampling, breaking down, stamping underfoot the plants and shrubs so lovingly tended by their owners. He relieved his feelings on some flourishing young cherry trees. Tore them up by the roots and flung them on the ground. This accomplished, he rushed on. As soon as he had vanished, two boys came out from behind the summerhouse. Schoolboys of twelve or so. Dizzy with excitement. They had been hiding there all the time. For them it was just an adventure. But if he had found them, God only knows what would have happened!

I couldn't help connecting the man on the balcony with the armed representative of law and order. They were two of a kind. In the behaviour of those two people there was such an enormous charge of pent-up hatred. First the man on the balcony: no Hercules – rather a weakling in fact, but he had handled the television set like a toy. Then this uprooter of trees.

The crowd in the street and the Zomo. It would be a fight to the death.

Hate welled up in me. I was ready.

The Well-Matched Couple

————————— * —————————

Wiesia and Dragal. What a couple! A splendid pair they made! If only because there was such a contrast between them. He was six foot with long hair and beard. His hair, sparse and greasy, straggled untidily down his neck. His whole appearance was a mess: clothes frayed, jeans and jacket patched and repatched, sandals on bare feet black with the dust of city streets, despite his assurances that he washed every day. Wiesia, on the other hand, was a tiny, dark-haired, delicate creature. Her tastes also ran to picturesque motley-gypsy skirts and Mexican ponchos. Wiesia is a divorced mother. She got divorced after meeting Dragal. Years ago. But they still behave like young lovers. They are nice, intelligent, and decent. In other words, the state of war hasn't got them down. Right from the start, despite the chaos and panic, they kept their heads. Went out, collected the news and before long were printing it. They acquired their skill before the present war, printing Solidarity's regional paper. They managed to save their equipment from the militia and stow it safely away. They started to print a bulletin, organized their distribution network carefully and were soon circulating a thousand copies at a time.

But their looks! Unusual, to say the least. Passers-by turned their heads. As for the police pack, the secret agents and the informers, Wiesia and Dragal were the answer to their prayers. Beards, dirt, rags meant students, conspirators, counter-revolutionaries. They were detained time after time. Luckily, nothing was ever found on them. But interrogation by all those patrols, raiding parties and night watches took up far too much of their time. They are not as young as all that.

They had their first taste of battle in 1968. At the start of their university careers. They had seen the inside of militia cells and a variety of jails. They had felt truncheons on their backs. With the years and their wide experience they grew tough. But they had kept their youthful looks. Especially Wiesia. Like a teenager, though she was well over thirty. Dragal is the same age. But after 13 December their defiant exoticism made them too conspicuous against our grey background. I met them for the first time about then. They knew the password. Wiesia came up to me first and gave it. Dragal followed. We went for a walk together and they made their proposal. I had copy. They had the means of printing it. Passers-by stared at us. I look dull and ordinary: light overcoat, plastic briefcase. And they were a couple of tattered, tousle-headed hippies. I confess that I didn't trust them completely. Yes, they knew the password, but they could have learnt it by chance. And they could have been planted. I didn't give them anything. Later on, I saw things more clearly and handed over some texts. But they began to be picked up more and more frequently. The checkpoint by the town hall hardly ever let them pass without asking for their documents. Searched their bags and frisked Dragal – legs, back, belly. People in our circle told them openly, 'Get yourselves tidied up. Cut your hair, shave, get hold of some normal clothes.' They smiled politely, nodded in agreement. And went on just as before. Stubborn as mules.

Things were hotting up. Strikes, demonstrations. Wiesia and Dragal were among the first to be rounded up: they landed at police headquarters and were kept there for a time. They were lucky not to be interned for their looks alone.

The Zomo couldn't take their eyes off them. Like cats after a mouse.

At the time our printing arrangements were in a state of chaos. We had managed to save some of the equipment. But we couldn't use it where it was. The risks were too great to make a move. Several printing teams had been arrested. Others had gone underground. But Wiesia and Dragal continued as before. They produced bulletins, leaflets, even pamphlets. They were without doubt the best team of our decimated force, overworked beyond belief. In the end, they asked for a few days' break and went off. By then rail traffic had returned to normal. They chose a picturesque old town in the south. A river, churches, a market square, arcaded streets. One of the few Polish towns to have preserved its original character. Much Renaissance and Baroque. It was Wiesia who made the choice – she was an art historian by training. They planned to spend four days away. Things went wrong from the start. As soon as they got off the train, they were challenged. Hostile eyes bored into them. Their documents were scrutinized. They were allowed to go. They walked towards the market square. Someone trailed along behind them. Dragal had an uneasy feeling but shrugged it off. Put it down to war nerves. They felt really free and easy. They hugged and they kissed. Because of the difference in height, Dragal's arm was round Wiesia's neck, and hers round his waist. They found a room easily enough, in an old hotel which remembered Franz Josef's day. They took their luggage up, had a bath and went out for a walk round the narrow streets of the old town. People in the street stared at them but they ignored this impertinent curiosity. They were used to it. They liked the place more and more. From the castle hill they could see the town and its approaches and the woods nearby. They walked into the gateway of a lovely old house to have a look at the courtyard with its galleries and its fountain, long dry. And this was where they were grabbed. First, Dragal, from behind. They twisted his arms behind his back. Then Wiesia. They pinned her to the wall. Uniformed police and plain-clothes men dragged them to headquarters.

'Obviously troublemakers. They may be wanted already,' said the plain-clothes man in charge of the operation as he led them into a room where an officer was sitting behind a desk.

They were searched again. Very thoroughly. Separately. Wiesia by a policewoman. The physical examination was very detailed indeed. The humiliation of it, and the brutality! Cross-examination followed. The officer and the other man took it in turn. Where had they come from? What was the purpose of their visit? A telephone call was made. Followed by a lot of whispering and a rustling of papers.

'What's it all about? What the hell do you want?' Dragal shouted. 'You have no right . . .'

'Keep your trap shut, you dirty bum,' roared the officer.

The grilling went on for hours. They were hungry and tired after the night train.

They were taken away and put in separate cells. Time passed. Dragal got thirsty. He banged on the door. A militiaman rushed in.

'I'll kick your balls in, you grubby bastard.' He brandished a bunch of keys threateningly.

Dragal desisted. He was very anxious about Wiesia. She had seemed so nervous lately. He suspected that she was pregnant. Hours passed. In the middle of the night they took him upstairs again. Wiesia wasn't there.

'Where is my wife?' asked Dragal.

'Wife, he says!' The officer found it funny. 'Concubine, he means!'

The other interrogator came into the room. Again they shared the questioning. Addresses? Contacts? Names?

Dragal stuck to his story.

'We came to look at the old town. My wife is an art historian and is writing about Polish Baroque.'

'Your concubine,' the interrogators doggedly corrected him. Then one of them sneeringly added:

'Your concubine's – sorry, your wife's – statement says something different. You're here to deliver illegal printed matter. Out to stir up trouble in a hard-working Polish town.'

Dragal didn't fall into the trap. He stopped answering and just shrugged his shoulders.

They spent forty-eight hours in the cells, and were released with a warning that they might be locked up for another forty-eight at any moment. Back in their hotel, they found that their luggage had been ransacked. The search had been thorough and nasty. Wiesia's clothes had been thrown around and trampled on. They packed in miserable silence and took the next train to Wroclaw.

I saw them soon afterwards. I honestly didn't recognize either of them at first. Dragal was clean-shaven, in a jacket and a well-pressed pair of trousers. A respectable middle-aged man. Wiesia was wearing an elegant, rather severe dress. They are different people, there's no denying it. They look considerably older nowadays.

But they are still doing their bit.

How Time Has Flown

———————————— ✳ ————————————

I used to enjoy football. In the forward line. Our team was called 'The Future'. Juniors. Even I got applause.

Dad was a train driver. Always on the go. A big stainless steel alarm clock stood on the sideboard to wake him up. Mum would have his food ready the night before. We wouldn't see him again for days. I was doing quite well at school. History and geography were my favourite subjects. At our singing lessons, I fell for the violin. Our singing teacher often played to us. Name of Giemza. Trained at the Conservatoire, violin class. Invited me to his house, taught me a bit. I could play, sort of. Giemza lived alone. I enjoyed my visits. Giemza talked. Don't remember what about. Chaps at school sniggered. Made faces, made gestures.

I didn't like being ridiculed. I had a fight with one of them. Can't remember who won. But I stopped seeing Giemza. I also avoided the boys. I hung around the church instead. They ran a drama society at the church hall. Put on short pieces and religious plays. Read poetry. I wasn't attracted to girls. Not for a long time. Ashamed and shy, I was. Girls eyed me on their way from the May masses. Giggled, laughed, lagged behind. I can still hear them. I should have dated a girl there and then. It didn't turn out that way. I wasn't keen enough on anyone. This went on so long that Mum complained about it. Father was dead by then. Died suddenly. On the way from work. Mum nagged and nagged. Started dragging up the story of the old singing teacher. That upset me quite a bit. I remember. My hands shook, there was a mist in front of my eyes, I nearly choked. Mum was scared. That teacher was a gentle, sensitive person. I went to work in an office. Stuck at it, intending to study in evening classes. It didn't work out. Cost too much. After the office I used to go out quite a bit. With friends from the office. To cafés where they had tea-dances – 'five o'clocks', they called them. The other chaps got married. Met the right girls at those dances or somewhere. I didn't. There were some I quite liked but it never came to anything. Mother stopped nagging. She got used to the way we lived. My brother moved out. She preferred living with me to being alone. I brought money in. I don't smoke. Drink very little. I like wine, especially sweet vermouth. I'm particular about my clothes. I like to look neat and fashionable. I used to have my shoes made for me because of fallen arches, but now I buy them ready made. I got fed up with those cafés. The music has changed. I don't like the rowdy modern stuff. I see less and less of my own age group. They stay at home with their wives, their children, and their duties. I used to be interested in the arts. Concerts, theatre, lectures. I started going to English classes. I haven't got the gift. My pronunciation is bad. Conversation is what really gets me down. But I go on with the lessons. Mother died. Old age. Quietly, in bed. I took care of the funeral, the gravestone. Buried next to my father, as she wished. It was funny, alone in the flat. Very quiet. Some people keep animals. I don't like dogs. Or cats. Mother kept a canary. He lived some time after her death. I looked after him. It felt very quiet, to begin with. In bed, I remember various occasions. Christmas. All the noise and running around. An aunt used to come, and a few other people. Later on my brother and his fiancée. I was born in this building, where I live now. The tenants have changed. I don't know the new ones. We say 'Good morning' on the stairs. I don't want a lodger. House isn't your own with strangers in it. I've gradually got used to the quiet. I like it now. I used to play chess with a neighbour sometimes. Passed the time in the evening. He died not long ago. An old man, very frail. Spent a long time in prisons – German, then Russian. Now I've developed a new interest. Polish history between the wars and during the Second World War. The truth. Not the official version. The actual sources. It's difficult to get at the truth. Honest books are very expensive. And mostly published abroad. I knew a man who went to the West on business. Promised to bring me some stuff, but didn't. Got scared. In the West they have archives, libraries, research institutes. I wrote to an old friend who lives in West Germany. Used to live near us. Eugeniusz, calls himself Eugen now. We were playmates. He wrote back. Sent a colour photo. Himself, wife, child, the house. A very nice detached house. He sent a Christmas card later. The correspondence petered out. What did I want from him? I don't really know. One life is very short, if you think of history. I used to be like other boys. Games, playing truant. I never thought then that I'd be left all alone, without wife or children. It was unimaginable. If the truth be told, I avoid my contemporaries. Everyone has a life of his own. I don't really need people, they wear you out, make demands on you. I prefer talking to old people. They're different. See things from a distance, through a mist. They don't moan all that much about what they have now and what they used to have. Settle down with somebody? I consider it sometimes. It could be one of the women I work with, or somebody who comes into my life unexpectedly. But nothing ever happens. Because of the singing teacher? No. I'm quite normal. But there's never been anybody I felt absolutely sure I wanted. I always have doubts, I'm scared of problems. People show themselves in their true colours only afterwards, they ask too much, throw their weight about. And I could never sleep in the same bed! Not even in the same room, not really. Well, maybe with Dolores. I wouldn't mind that. Came from Venezuela. Raven-haired. We met in a cinema: I translated the Polish dialogue into English for her. Why did she take such a liking to me? Maybe because I'm fair. Going bald, but still fair. She was sorry to leave. Sent me an invitation. Was it serious on my side? I'm not sure. It would mean travelling to strange places. I was refused a passport. I appealed but lost. She wrote a few times. Then it was over. I think about Venezuela from time to time. A nice fairy tale. I have one big room and a kitchen. Prewar building. Very airy, warm. Sunny. Only difficult to get enough coal to last you through the winter. Well, time does fly. So quickly! Faster and faster! I've lived quite a time, really. My father was dead at my age! I look back and can't see any sense in it all. I mean any real force deciding which way things go. Life just rolls by. I simply don't know why things happen as they do. At one time I could always find something to look forward to. Last time it was the passport I was waiting for. Gave my imagination something to work on. Something good would drop in my lap. I was waiting for something. Maybe I'm still waiting? I don't think so. Peace and quiet, that's all I want. Go home, eat something – I cook for myself – tidy the flat, wash some underwear, listen to the radio, read a book . . and it's time for bed. Life is running by.

God? Immortality? I'm not sure. I read a lot. I've ruined my eyes. I have to change glasses every year. I forget things. Keep going back to the old days. I remember them best. I go to bed at ten, regularly. Sleep won't come. It's all nonsense! They bury you and that's that. But I'm afraid – there's this fear inside me. It was always there, and I've always hidden like a snail in its shell. It's getting worse. My resistance gets lower as time goes by. Those blue lights, or are they purple? Signals of death? Revolving on the house tops. And the sirens. Jangle your nerves. The rumble of tanks. Down in the street, over the cobbles, the noise reverberates. An endless procession of them. But the purple lights are worst. I remember the Occupation and the first years after the war. I was young then. They took some people and killed some others. Father had to stay in hiding for a time. History repeats itself, they say. The noise comes right into the flat, you can't escape it. My treatment doesn't help me any longer. It used to. The priest from Grebkowo prescribed it. Herbal medicine. There were crowds besieging the presbytery. I waited the whole day, told him about my head. The priest said my nerves were bad. The malady of our time, he called it. Prescribed treatment: very simple. Take half a glass of water, five teaspoonfuls of vodka, three teaspoonfuls of vinegar and half a tablespoonful of salt. Rub your back with it. Every night. It used to help, but it doesn't any more. I listen from my bed waiting for a convoy to come past. They come every night at the same time. I look around my walls. Here they come. The rumble. The deathly lights. They've gone. I get up. Walk from my room to the kitchen. Mementoes of a long life. Father's railway uniform. I keep it in mothballs. An album. My parents when they were young. Father, with his mates, by a locomotive. Me and my brother. In shorts and sailor collars. Things like that. An iron, shaped like a heart. Belonged to mother. What did it all mean? I don't know, I can't sleep. I must go and see the priest at Grebkowo again. I dare say they'll give me a pass. I'm sorry I never managed to see that healer, Harris. Harris cures by touch. Maybe, if he touched me . . .

The Search

———————————*———————————

They went to town today. Especially with the young. But anybody with a bag or rucksack was sure to be stopped.

The checkpoint behind the church of the Holy Ghost was the worst. A mixed lot, militia and army. Wouldn't let anybody through. They had sharp eyes and the devil's own flair. When a peasant with a sack came along they took one look and waved him through. Didn't even watch him go. They were never in two minds. A minute later, a young man with a child appeared. Taking his little girl for a walk. He had a haversack over his shoulder. An innocent looking green haversack. He was almost past the checkpoint.

'Hold on a moment!' That was the militiaman with the dark moustache and two stripes on his sleeve. Had a gypsy look about him. Cat-like, unhurried, he approached the young father. Kalashnikov hanging round his neck, right hand on the trigger. Moving in for the kill. He opened the green bag and went through it skilfully and thoroughly. Took some papers out. A typewritten sheaf of flimsies slipped under the foil round a packet of veg. The corporal's eyes brightened. He hustled the young father under the arches, where the officer in charge was sitting, and rushed back to bag another victim. He scored more than all the rest of them put together. A few minutes later, he stopped a young girl, and an old man leaning on a stick. Found something on each of them. The old man was cunning. He was carrying a bulging briefcase, with nothing of interest in it. The corporal was too smart for him though. He worked steadily through the man's pockets and found it. A leaflet. He looked pretty pleased with himself.

The army were less keen. But they had to make some sort of effort. The corporal with the moustache took time off now and then to watch them with his bright black eyes. He missed nothing. The army had to keep at it.

They divided the street between them: the soldiers hunted on the left, the militia on the right.

The corporal finished a cigarette and got to work again. Three girl students came strolling along, arm in arm, laughing and carefree. But the corporal wasn't taken in. He stopped them and gutted their handbags.

Almost simultaneously, one of the soldiers stopped a girl. She was by herself. Wearing very thick glasses. She must have had very poor sight. She walked right up to the young soldier and he couldn't help stopping her. He didn't seem very good at the job. Fumbled with frozen fingers in her white Coca Cola bag till a make-up case dropped out. He picked it up quickly, mumbled 'Sorry'. What a bashful soldier! In the end, he dug out a pamphlet in green covers. Obviously illicit. One of those pamphlets the free press used to put out before this war. Still does, for all I know. He extracted it from her bag and looked around furtively.

The gypsy – the militia corporal I mean – was still tied up with his female trio. The others were busy too. The whole bunch had gathered round a tall man with a black hat, carrying a big suitcase. They all wanted to have a go at it.

Another shifty look around and the young soldier dropped the green pamphlet into the Coke bag.

'Thank you. You may go,' he told the girl.

She just stood there. Obviously flabbergasted. Red as a beetroot. Then she moved off, too fast. Very inexperienced.

But nobody noticed.

The Shadow

————————— * —————————

I had some important papers on me. Reports from Silesia. The most important was an account of the strike in the Wujek mine, from one of the participants. A guy had just brought it over. A tiny roll of flimsy paper, stuffed into a ballpoint pen. That's what we've come to. Read about the Occupation in anybody's memoirs – it's all there. I thought it safest to slip the stuff into my sock, right down inside my shoe. Seemed like a good idea. Just in case. I haven't been blown, but better safe than sorry, as they say. And the night before, when the boys rang me, they had spoken openly about the meeting, although the call was monitored.

'We meet at Jurek's. As always. You know the time.'

I said yes and put down the receiver straightaway. What on earth had got into them! There was no need to remind me. In that giveaway style! All those dark hints! Save me from amateur conspirators.

I got on an express bus. It stopped at the square. I got off and decided to walk to the next stop, outside the cinema, and catch a tram or a bus from there. I looked both ways. And behind. Several people were walking in the same direction. It was raining a bit. And suddenly the skies burst. The pavement was slippery. I had been walking slowly, as though I was out for a stroll. Not a very bright idea. In weather like that? I speeded up. The going was difficult. I slipped once. Almost lost my balance. My feet wanted to go different ways.

There was only one person behind me now. Man or

woman? I couldn't see a thing. I heard a curse. A man's voice. Must have slipped. I reached the cinema. Closed down. 'Only pigs go to the pics' – that was a slogan during the Occupation. I stopped in the bus shelter. Not many waiting. An elderly couple. Some teenagers. Neutral kind of people. Then a couple with a kid. The rain beat more and more heavily on the glass roof. Someone else stopped near the shelter. Didn't come inside despite the rain. A man. The streetlight was reflected in his glasses. His face was invisible, his collar was up. He paced up and down impatiently. A few steps this way. A few steps that. Had he been following me? Was this the man? I couldn't be sure. The bus, when it came, was packed. I waited till it moved and jumped onto the platform. The rear platform. The man got on from the front. Also at the last moment. Interesting? Very. There was such a crush you couldn't move. I could feel the papers against my ankle, hidden inside my boot. Who would ever look there, even in a frisk? Usually, they just go through your pockets. Four stops later, at the new estate, I got off. Should've gone on to the next stop, but this seemed safer. Somehow, I managed to shoulder my way out of the bus. I looked round. There was someone behind me. I stopped. He stopped. Let's see who can keep it up longest. I waited patiently. He was very close. I crept forward like a ballet dancer, then retreated. He was wearing most unsuitable shoes, with highish heels. Had to slither along like a dancer on ice. He stopped. I saw glasses glint again. The same man? He bent down to do something to his shoe. I had to give in. He was behind me again. Evidently, he wasn't new to the job. I passed three high-rise buildings at an angle to the road and came to allotments. No streetlights. Darkness. The first allotment had a fence round it. Luckily the gate was open. I sneaked in and crouched behind a shed. Steps. A crash. Must have slipped. Maybe fallen? Steps again. Then silence. I stuck my head out through the gate. No-one in sight. Right, I decided, take a parallel street, just in case. Then turn at the lay-by. It worked. I wanted the fourth building on the right. Steps again. Just when I wasn't expecting them. I stood, waiting, by a telephone box. Not a sound. What was it, for Christ's sake? Someone going to the dustbin? Or out with the dog? I was getting ridiculously jumpy. My own shadow on the wall seemed to belong to someone else. The fourth building. The first staircase. The first floor. I flew up the stairs and rang the bell. Quick steps behind. Should I run up to the next floor? Or down? Too late. The door opened wide. The occupant of the flat stood there smiling.

'You're right on time. Splendid.'

I raised a warning finger to my lips.

The man I'd seen downstairs was just behind me. The same man, I thought. Glasses glinted.

'Excellent. Both right on time. Let me introduce you.'

I looked blank. So did he.

'I thought you . . .'

'And I thought *you* . . .'

We shook hands.

A New Life

————————— ✳ —————————

A deserted country lane. A man stood at the roadside. Trying to support a woman writhing in pain. Dogs barked from cottages nearby, answering her wild screams. The man felt helpless. The pains had started at midnight, never let go. They seemed to be getting worse. He watched anxiously. Her eyes glistened. She was crying.

They had been standing at the crossroads for a long time. Ten kilometres to the nearest town, the hospital. For one short moment he felt hopeful. Stared into the oncoming lights. Flung out his arms, shouted. The car passed them without slowing down. His eyes followed the receding lights in despair. He cursed in a whisper.

There was a momentary silence now. The woman had stopped screaming. She was breathing hard. The breathing was irregular, feverish.

'Are you better?' he asked, uncertainly.

She shook her head. She hung heavily on him. He stared into the darkness again. Trying to watch all four roads at once. The fields were white. The sky hung black and starless over the earth. The woman cried out. The sound was magnified by the silence. The dogs started barking again. He couldn't see her face. But he could hear the grinding of her teeth and see the huge belly protruding from the folds of her coat.

Lights from the right. They grew brighter. He sat her down on a pile of stones and rushed into the middle of the road. The truck driver jammed on his brakes. The truck travelled for another few metres on the slippery surface. A hail of oaths came from the driver's cab. The man ran back to collect his companion. He took her in his arms, bending under her weight. He carried her to the truck, climbed on the step.

'Hospital. As fast as you can.'

The driver opened the door, helped him to lay her down on the seat. She moaned continuously.

The driver started the engine and moved off so abruptly that the back wheels skidded. He didn't speak. The cab felt warm. The radio was on. The pennants pinned above the mirror fluttered as though in a wind. The man sighed with relief.

'Thank you, mate,' he said.

The driver pushed a packet of cigarettes towards him. His fingers were so stiff that it took time to ease one out. He smoked feverishly.

'What's wrong with her?' the driver asked. A young voice. The light fell on his face as they passed a streetlamp. Three days' growth of beard, deep shadows under the eyes.

'Labour pains,' the man answered, looking at the woman's pale sweaty face. She was breathing with difficulty.

'I'll step on it. We'll be there very soon.'

The ramshackle old truck pushed on at a speed it was unused to. The engine coughed and the whole vehicle creaked and rattled.

'It's an old crock, but it does what it's told,' said the driver complacently.

They were stopped by a strong light in their faces. The driver lowered his head, instinctively. The light blinded him. The road was barred by a motorcycle with a sidecar. Two militiamen waved their automatics threateningly.

'Animals,' barked the driver.

The truck braked with difficulty and stopped right in front of the motorcycle.

'Traffic check,' said one militiaman.

'You drive too fast,' added the other one, massaging his frostbitten ears.

The driver gave them his papers. The militiaman turned his torch onto the couple in the cab.

'I'm taking them to the hospital. Picked them up at the roadside.'

The woman moaned.

The militiaman watched her for quite a time.

'Your papers.'

The man rummaged in his pockets. Found his wallet at last.

The militiaman thumbed the pages of his identity document. Read out the name of the district he lived in.

'What are you doing at this time of night?' The torch lit the man's face. He blinked.

'Oh God!' he whispered, his hands tightly pressed on his knees.

The driver answered instead:

'As I said, I'm taking them to the hospital.'

The other militiaman looked into the body of the truck from the rear. He lifted the tarpaulin. The truck was full of neatly arranged sacks.

'Potatoes, for the factory,' said the driver. 'Two tons.'

The militiaman felt the sacks. Slowly, with care. The first one gave the driver back his papers but kept the passengers'.

'What about her?' He pointed at the woman.

The man was stroking her hand. Gently, he moved her head.

'She may die any minute,' the driver volunteered.

The militiaman mumbled something. But he let it go. Didn't repeat the question. Gave the man his papers. The man shuddered, suddenly, and uttered a strange inarticulate sound. The driver squeezed his arm.

'Okay in the back?' the first militiaman asked his partner, who was checking the sacks of potatoes. He turned a powerful beam on the back of the truck. 'Hasn't got anything in there?' he added, with sudden suspicion.

'Clean,' answered the other. He let down the tarpaulin. Brushed down his tunic carefully, with a gloved hand.

The first militiaman turned off his torch. Kicked the front tyre with a heavy boot.

'Not enough air,' he remarked, and yawned. 'Get going!'

The driver switched on the ignition. The engine fired. And stalled. He tried again. They could hear the militia talking. Laughter reached them through the coughing and spluttering of the engine. At last the engine started properly. The truck moved off. The driver pushed his cigarettes towards the man. They lit up.

The man wiped some sweat from her forehead. Her head lolled back.

'Asleep.'

When he looked again he realized that she was unconscious.

'Quick!' he shouted, 'Quick!'

He felt scared: they would lose the child. She would have a miscarriage. It would be stillborn.

He started praying, trying to remember words long-forgotten.